ROWENA
STEIN

A gripping Victorian historical
mystery with romance

TON EMMES

ROWENA STEIN: A GRIPPING VICTORIAN HISTORICAL MYSTERY WITH ROMANCE

First edition. June 8, 2024.

Copyright © 2024 TON EMMES.

ISBN: 979-8227341723

Written by TON EMMES.

One

London, 1847

Beads of sweat trickled down his pale forehead. Eyes wide with fear, he fixated his gaze on my delicate hand attempting to draw blood from the vein in his arm. He rolled his eyes back. A slight dizziness overwhelmed his senses, he seemed on the verge of fainting. Perhaps it was the sight of the metal syringe I wielded, or maybe he thought all the blood in his body would drain out through the small hole the needle had made.

While I was focused on the bloodletting I was performing, I noticed my father behind me, worried and desperate to take the syringe from my hands.

I drew back the syringe plunger, and the red fluid began to flow into the metal body of the device. I had carried out this procedure several times before, always with my father's assistance. This was the first time I was doing it all by myself, hence his concern looming over me.

Max, the person from whom I was drawing blood, was our butler. At that moment, his face was pale, and he was sweating profusely. Not being particularly brave, he always panicked at the sight of the needle inserted into his arm.

"Hold on a moment, Rowena Duncan Stein. Max is terribly frightened. This blood sample is sufficient. I see you've learned the whole process," my father said, interrupting me before our butler could faint. "Next, I'll teach you how to perform a blood transfusion, it's still an experimental area in the scientific community here in London, but I'm keen for you to learn. You've shown a great deal of interest in medicine.

Dr. Robert Duncan Stein, my father, was a respected surgeon and professor. At just 16 years of age, I harbored an immense curiosity to learn everything related to his work. He had guided me in learning first aid, and blood extraction was part of these teachings. Of course, he was fully aware that the education of young ladies in our era was limited to learning good manners, music, sewing, embroidery, and painting to become accomplished, and find a suitable match for marriage. I disagreed with these outdated notions that institutions imposed on us. At least, not at this time, and he knew it. My thoughts were directed towards someday being able to help sick people, as he did, and perhaps one day when our society permits, I could become a great doctor. My father didn't suppress this desire; on the contrary, he encouraged me, allowing me to assist him with some of his patients, for practice.

His office was in our house in Gordon Square, Bloomsbury. From my bedroom window, I could see the beautiful garden that the vast square presented to me every morning. My father was very strict about asepsis in his work, something that wasn't common among doctors of our time. Some of his colleagues even teased him, saying that Dr. Robert would be considered a forerunner of a new era in medicine. My father dreaded losing any patient to germs, bacteria, or other microorganisms. He sought to instill this same work philosophy in his students at the medical school of St Bartholomew Hospital, or Barts as the locals nicknamed it.

Max, having recovered from his fright, went to answer the door. One of our servants informed us that the police inspector wished to speak with Dr. Robert.

"Max, take him to my study," my father said.

As a doctor, my father had collaborated with Inspector Peter Tennyson on several occasions. I personally found the inspector to be rude and insolent. I don't know how my father tolerated such disrespect. Especially him, who was meticulous about social norms, especially with me and my sister Emily Duncan Stein.

I left the office and was passing in front of his study, which door was slightly ajar. When the inspector spoke:

"She was found nearly drained of blood. I need your guidance."

"Drained of blood?"

My steps froze. I couldn't move. There was an internal struggle. To be a nosy parker – which wasn't how I'd been raised – or to remain indifferent to what I had just heard.

Of course, my youthful recklessness prevailed. I swear I didn't try to eavesdrop further, but I needed to know who the victim was. I stayed close enough to the study door to hear the rest of the conversation, praying not to get caught red-handed.

"Dr. Robert, she was very young, probably no older than sixteen. Please, we can't waste much time. She's still where we found her, and the place is crawling with onlookers. Including your meddlesome friend Mr. Fawcett," said the inspector with his usual lack of subtlety.

"I agree Inspector. I'll grab my medical bag in case I need to examine the victim. And as for young Mr. Thomas Fawcett, he's just doing his job."

"Fine. As long as he doesn't get in my way."

I heard noises of chairs being moved; they were leaving. I walked quickly to the office, next to the study, pretending I was still tidying up the instruments I had used on Max. My father grabbed his medical bag, bid farewell, and left with the inspector.

Concerned about the conversation I had overheard in the office, I walked towards the library. It was a spacious room, with shelves full of books that covered the walls. Most of them were about medicine, including some rare specimens, the rest were there to foster learning for Emily and me. Two armchairs and a sofa with a small table, on a thick carpet, surrounded the fireplace. As usual, I found my sister Emily, sprawled on one of the sofas with a copy of Punch, a magazine of humor and satire, which dad disapproved of us flipping through. I picked up the day's newspaper from the tray on the small table, beside the sofa where my father sat. He hadn't even had time to read it yet, so I sat down and started to leaf through it carefully. Dr. Robert hated it when we read newspapers, especially before he did. I was looking for any mention of the murder, which the inspector had mentioned.

"You know dad doesn't like us reading newspapers," said my annoying sister.

"And he doesn't approve of you reading this kind of magazine either," I told her, as Emily grimaced at me.

Emily was two years younger, a tad taller, and much prettier. Much prettier. Our mother had passed away during Emily's birth, as dad had told us. It was a difficult delivery, she was very feverish when she gave birth to my sister, and could not withstand the pains inflicted upon her by Emily's birth. Dad was deeply shaken by her death. He still blames himself to this day, that as a doctor, he couldn't save his own wife. Perhaps that's why he never remarried.

He practically raised us on his own. I grew up and became a young woman, and in two years would be introduced to society. His attention towards me was doubled, I believe he was afraid that I might fall prey to some libertine. Emily thought that dad blamed her for our mother's death, of course, that wasn't true. We had tried everything to get this idea out of her head, but she didn't understand, which is why she thought dad favored me over her. She was always creating situations to irritate me. Taking my dresses and personal items without my permission. That's when she wasn't concocting some gossip with dad using my name.

I didn't pay much mind to what Emily said, after all, she was also reading something forbidden, and returned to reading the newspaper. I combed through the tabloid from cover to cover, and found nothing about the murder. Of course, there were various crimes, robberies, and other horrors, but not what I was looking for. Perhaps it would only come out in tomorrow's newspaper.

That's why my father didn't allow us to read newspapers. He wanted to shield us from so much of humanity's filth.

I placed the newspaper back on the tray, exactly as I found it. Then I heard Max opening the door of the vestibule for my father. From the voices, he had a visitor with him. I looked at Emily, who straightened up on the sofa, hiding her copy of Punch under a cushion. We didn't recognize the voice accompanying him.

"Max, where are the girls?" asked dad.

"In the library, sir."

My father appeared at the entrance of the library, next to our unknown visitor. He was a tall, elegant, handsome man, with honey-colored eyes, thick black hair, and he wore a beautifully cut black coat.

"Rowena Stein, Emily Duncan. This is Mr. Thomas Fawcett. A friend and collaborator. As it happens, he was also at the scene of a murder."

"How odd. Your collaborator in what, dad?"

"A murder, how dreadful," said Emily, making a face of disgust.

He approached, removed one of his gloves, and came in my direction, but my sister stood up too quickly, losing her balance and almost falling into his arms. He found himself greeting her first and, then me, who remained seated. When he greeted me, he bowed slightly and looked deep into my eyes, leaving me feeling momentarily uncomfortable. He offered me his hand, we weren't close enough for this familiarity, but I decided to extend mine, to spare him any embarrassment in front of my father. He held the tips of my fingers gently and pressed them lightly.

"Delighted, Miss Stein," he said, smiling from one corner of his lips.

"Thomas, let's go to my office. I need to know more details about this young woman murdered."

"I do too. But how?"

Mr. Fawcett bid farewell and followed my father to his office.

"Did you see Rowena, how he looked at me?"

"Don't be ridiculous, Emily, he just greeted you, barely looked at you."

Memories of my childhood sometimes popped into my mind. Emily and I were raised by our father, and on certain occasions, our Aunt Annie, who was still a young girl of thirteen or fourteen at the time, provided the feminine presence in our home, along with our nanny, when he had to attend a medical conference in another city and we were still very young. But for most of our childhood, we were lovingly cared for by Nanny Abby, who passed away two years ago. It was a deep stab in our hearts. Emily spent a whole day and night sobbing her heart out, as she had always seen the nanny as a substitute mother. I believe Emily's temperament began to change after Abby's death. Poor sister, she blamed herself for our mother's death during childbirth, and then lost the nanny we dearly loved. These two losses made Emily grow bitter towards people, including me. Frivolity took over her being, and love and affection started to dwindle in her heart. Sometimes she would let her guard down and show bursts of tenderness or even gratitude, towards me or our father. But soon, a fog would again veil her soul. I tried everything to make her happy. Almost always, I would step aside, during outings or parties, letting her wear a better dress or a prettier hat so that she could shine at the events. That was my biggest mistake. Emily developed a very strong narcissistic personality. Her life revolved around her beauty—indeed, she was very beautiful. And she thought all men would fall at her feet. She was quite young, and life would probably hurt her a lot if she saw her appearance as the way to pave her path. Our society would not forgive her. I tried to warn her several times, but she always thought I was jealous of her beauty. Deep down, I knew that all this behavior stemmed from a lack of maternal affection. That's why I tried to tolerate it. Father should have remarried.

The curtains of my room were flung open abruptly, and I woke up startled. Gradually, I was able to make out the silhouette of my sister, contrasting with the morning light streaming through the window of my room.

"What happened, Emily?" I asked, still sleepy.

"You promised to accompany me to the dressmaker's today. Remember? I need to have some new dresses made."

"But you have so many dresses! And all stunning, to boot."

"They're for the upcoming dance season."

"Emily, you're too young to fuss about these balls. The dresses you have are more than enough. Besides, I have a piano lesson this morning."

"It doesn't matter! You agreed to go with me. Cancel the lesson, you don't even like those lessons anyway."

"Did Father authorize new clothes?"

"Yes. Why wouldn't he authorize it?"

As much as possible, Father indulged our whims, especially Emily's. I believe it was his way of compensating for the absence of our mother. Being the oldest, I helped him take care of my sister, as his day was short for so many tasks. Managing a home, two teenage daughters, teaching, and attending to his patients.

I had breakfast with Emily. I asked Max to prepare the carriage; we were going to the dressmaker's and shopping.

Burlington Arcade on Piccadilly was a gallery with a majestic three-arch entrance, housing a large display of shops inside. With a variety of merchants, including some fine establishments run by foreigners. There were flower, jewelry, shoe, dressmaker's, hat shops, bookstores, and print shops. I asked our coachman to stop in front of its entrance and come back after two hours. Emily and I were going to window shop. My sister, excited by the novelties, wanted to buy everything; I controlled her as best as I could. Poor father.

As we were passing a hat shop, unexpectedly, a couple coming out of the store collided with us. They were still absorbed in their conversation.

"Miss Stein, Miss Duncan. My apologies for the incident. We were so caught up in our conversation," said Mr. Thomas Fawcett with a smile.

There was Mr. Fawcett, his arm linked with a young lady's, a stunning young lady, actually. I don't know why, but seeing Thomas being intimate next to that girl, I felt embarrassed and looked down at the ground. Emily, on the other hand, was direct and sarcastic.

"Hello! Mr. Fawcett. Why don't you introduce us to your girlfriend?"

He laughed and commented.

"Girlfriend? No. This is Joanna Fawcett, my sister. She was helping me pick out a new hat."

Joanna was tall with a slim silhouette, and she graced us with a charming smile. We smiled back at her, and after the introductions, Mr. Fawcett and his sister decided to accompany us to the dressmaker's. I was hesitant, but Emily, with her youthful enthusiasm, convinced me.

While Emily and the dressmaker were choosing fabrics and taking her new measurements, the conversation between Mr. Fawcett and me flowed casually. He seemed to be a pleasant person to talk to, a bit snobbish, but bearable. His sister hardly intervened in the subjects, not wanting to interrupt her brother's conversation.

We left the dressmaker's, and our carriage was already waiting for us; we said our goodbyes. Mr. Fawcett helped me into the carriage, lingering longer than etiquette allowed. I quickly pulled my hand away. He bowed and smiled. Leaning back against the cushioned seat, my heart racing, I gave the driver the order. And the carriage departed.

Two

"Run, Daddy, the village is on fire. We're going to die," I screamed in my father's arms as behind us our village was ablaze. I couldn't see my mother, but I felt she was close. Houses were on fire. People being burned alive. Children crying. It was a living hell. And my father ran with me in his arms, reaching back trying to hold the hand of someone running with us. Mom.

"Miss. Miss Stein," someone called to me from afar.

Startled, I woke up. It was my maid Lucy, trying to wake me.

"You were having nightmares again. You were very agitated. That's why I woke you."

"Thank you, Lucy. I had that awful nightmare again. Is my father at home?"

"No, Miss. He went to the hospital."

"Ask Mary Penny to prepare my coffee, I'm going out."

"The housekeeper left. I will prepare your breakfast myself."

"Where did she go?" I asked, annoyed. Lately, Mary had been going out a lot without explanation. I needed to check into this.

"I don't know, Miss. Maybe Max knows."

I got up. Lucy helped me choose what to wear. I went downstairs to have my coffee that she had prepared. I wasn't hungry. My stomach was in knots because of the distress the nightmare caused me.

I needed to talk to my father, maybe he could explain why I was having such a recurrent dream. Max also didn't know where Mary Penny had gone. I wasn't in the mood to think about her now, I would resolve this issue with the housekeeper later. I asked Max to prepare the carriage for my departure. The dream had left me restless.

The Barts where my father was a professor and surgeon, was located near West Smithfield. A beautiful statue of King Henry VIII stood above its main gate. I got out of the carriage, entered the entrance hall and began climbing the stairs, stopping to admire on the wall, as I always did, the two beautiful murals painted by the artist William Hogarth. The painting The Pool of Bethesda, I took particular interest in, and I believe so did all the hospital's doctors, it showed a scene where Christ healed the sick. And I speculated about what diseases Christ's patients were suffering from. I finished climbing the stairs and looked for my father's office. Having been there several times before, it was easy to find. In the anteroom, a gentleman was talking to my father's assistant. Hearing my steps, he turned around. It was Mr. Thomas Fawcett.

I froze.

"How handsome he is!"

"Good morning, Miss Stein. A pleasure to see you again," he said, with joy in his eyes.

I greeted the assistant and turned my attention to him.

"Good morning, Mr. Fawcett. I came to speak with my father."

"Me too, but it seems he is in a meeting with Dr. Henry Holyhead, the hospital director."

"Then I'll speak with him at home. I didn't expect him to be so busy."

"Please, Miss Stein, wait a little while. The director will be out soon, and Dr. Robert will be very cross with me if I let you go without seeing him," said the assistant, anxiously.

At that moment, my father's office door opened. He came out accompanied by a tall man, well-built, wearing a neat black coat, and a tall, slender lady, slightly bent over probably from the pains her body inflicted on her, supported by a delicate mahogany cane.

"Dr. Henry and Mrs. Gertie, this is my daughter, Rowena Stein."

"She's a lovely young lady, Dr. Robert. Congratulations," said the lady with a slight smile.

I thanked her. She said goodbye to me and Mr. Fawcett and left. My father offered me his arm, and we entered his office.

"Thomas, excuse me, it's just a moment, and we'll talk," said my father to Thomas, who nodded in agreement.

My father's office was very spacious. It had shelves on the wall, with several volumes, all well bound. I sat down in a leather-upholstered chair in front of his large mahogany desk.

I told him about the terrible dream I had. And I asked him, not as a father but as a doctor, to explain why these nightmares recurred, each time leaving me more terrified, as real as they seemed.

"When there's an incident that leaves a deep impression on the mother during pregnancy or even at the time of our birth, these issues can become amplified in our youth, often chasing us into adulthood. Rowena, I believe your nightmares could be rooted in some significant event that occurred at your birth."

"But what could have been so terrible about my birth that I'm haunted by such horrific dreams?" I asked, visibly distressed. "I can't recall any event. Our life has always been peaceful."

"I wish you wouldn't worry so much about this. They are just dreams, which might not even be related to you. I promise to look into it. If I find anything that could be linked to these dreams, I'll let you know. For now, just be patient; I believe time will reveal the answers you're seeking."

My father stood up, opened the office door, and called for Thomas:

"Thomas, would you kindly escort my daughter home? She's quite shaken. If you don't mind, we'll talk another time."

"Of course he wouldn't mind. The twinkle in his eyes said it all."

"It would be my pleasure to escort your daughter. And of course, our conversation can wait for another time."

Mr. Fawcett helped me into the carriage and sat opposite me.

"Dr. Robert mentioned you're feeling nervous. Can I help in any way?"

"I doubt it. I've been plagued by nightmares recently. They feel so real!"

"Indeed, a night of poor sleep can really mess you up the next day."

"Mr. Fawcett, is it just me, or was there a hidden meaning in what you just said?"

Not liking where the conversation was headed, I decided to bring up the topic that interested me.

"Are you a doctor? My father introduced you as one of his colleagues."

"No, I'm a journalist. My family owns The Express newspaper," he said with a smile. "As for working with your father, I'd prefer he explain that part."

"Damn, what is he hiding?"

The traffic was quite congested that morning, allowing our carriage to only crawl along, giving me the chance to probe Mr. Fawcett further.

"You were at a crime scene yesterday. Is that part of your job as a journalist?"

"Yes, one of them. I'm an investigative journalist, and being young, I'm always on the lookout for new challenges. Please, Rowena, call me Thomas, after all, I'm only three years older than you," Thomas said as he took my hand in his, which I quickly withdrew to avoid blushing.

"Please, Mr. Fawcett," I said, feeling embarrassed, and changed the subject. "And that poor girl found yesterday. Can you tell me anything about her?"

"She had been medically examined by your father the day before. She was the daughter of a nurse who works with Dr. Robert. The police found one of his prescriptions in the victim's purse."

"Are they accusing my father?"

"I don't think so. They just came to ask him for medical advice and information about the victim, since Dr. Robert knew her. And because she was found completely drained of blood, with a deep cut on her neck, the inspector sought your father's help. They don't understand how the blood was removed. They're considering the possibility of it being the work of some dark magic ritual."

"Dark Magic?"

"Of course not! The police are just clutching at straws. Anything they can't logically explain, they attribute to some ritual. Why this interest in the murder?" Thomas asked. "It was so brutal."

"Maybe because she was as young as I am. It shook me. Also, out of medical curiosity, I wished I could have seen the body, to try and understand how the blood was removed."

"You're studying medicine?"

"For now, just with my father while I assist him with his patients. I intend to become a doctor, when it's allowed."

We arrived at my residence, and since Thomas was late for an appointment, I asked my coachman to take him. He gave me his business card with his address. I thanked Thomas for his company and the card, and he informed me he'd return in the afternoon as he had unfinished business with my father.

"Why would a young man like Thomas be so involved with my father?"

Three

Max opened the door for me, bearing good news. My Aunt Annie had returned from her travels and would be joining us for afternoon tea, as she often did when she wasn't off exploring.

I adored Aunt Annie. She was young, beautiful, and stylish, yet sometimes her visits could be a bit dull. She and Emily would only talk about the ball season, potential suitors, gossip, and, of course, the latest corset styles. I despised corsets. Despite this, I always joined these gatherings as a way for us to catch up, and usually, some silly remark would make me chuckle.

Mary Penny and the maid, as always, prepared a delightful spread of fruit tarts, biscuits, and cakes, all delicious, laid out on a table covered with a beautiful embroidered linen cloth, accompanied by an elegant tea set.

Aunt Annie was wearing an elegant flowered taffeta dress. I couldn't fathom why she was still unmarried; I believe men didn't appreciate forthright and independent women like her. A woman's honest voice seemed to bother them.

I had been chatting and taking tea with Auntie and Emily for some time when Max excused himself and announced that Mr. Thomas Fawcett was in the living room waiting for me.

I was startled, the cup I was holding fell from my hand. I wasn't quick enough to catch it before it hit the floor. It shattered, and one of the shards cut my finger. I quickly grabbed one of the embroidered napkins from the table, pressed it against the cut, and hurried to the restroom.

"Rowena, what happened? Did you cut yourself?" Aunt Annie asked.

I couldn't respond to her; I was already in the restroom, washing my hands and cleaning the blood, as the cut had already healed, leaving no scar.

"Not again, nobody can know about my gift."

I returned to the tea room, finding Thomas, Emily, and Auntie chatting merrily.

"Miss Stein, your sister took the liberty of going to the living room and inviting me for a cup of tea. Was your injury severe?"

"Emily, always taking the initiative."

"No, it was just a minor scratch. It's not even visible anymore. I was just startled by the breaking cup," I lied.

Our maid had cleaned up the shards, and Thomas was seated in the chair next to mine. He stood up and pulled out the chair for me to sit, his hand brushed mine. My heart raced; we were so close. A warmth started to rise through my entire body.

"Father hasn't arrived yet," I said as I recovered.

"Max informed me. He should be here soon. I'm a bit early. Would you mind keeping me company while I wait for Dr. Robert?"

Aunt Annie seemed to read between the lines of Thomas's words, that he wanted to be alone with me. She stood up at once.

"I'm sorry, Mr. Fawcett, Emily and I can't keep you company. I've returned from a trip this week, and Emily is eager to see the new things and the gifts I brought. Isn't that right, Emily?"

"What? Of course...new things?" Emily stammered nonsensically.

"It's not like that, Aunt. It's just a friendship starting."

Emily and Aunt Annie climbed the stairs toward the bedrooms, and I invited Thomas to join me in the library room. Thomas, with his upright posture and gentlemanly bearing, followed me. We sat down in comfortable leather armchairs, facing each other, and he smiled.

"Thank you for keeping me company, and I apologize for interrupting your tea."

"Don't worry about it. We had finished; we were just shooting the breeze."

"This morning, you seemed interested in seeing the body of the murdered girl."

"Yes. Why?"

"The young woman's body is at the St. Thomas Hospital morgue. During the day, only doctors have access. At night, I can manage to dodge the surveillance, but it would be dangerous for a young lady like yourself. Moreover, your father would have my head if he found out. He would think I'm tarnishing his daughter's reputation."

Thomas had a cheeky way of speaking, but I confess I was beginning to feel attracted to him. The invitation to go out alone at night did not feel disrespectful to me, as I believed he just wanted to help. Yet, at the same time, I felt scared, scared of venturing out in the early hours with a man I barely knew. Especially to visit a morgue, at night. I don't even want to think what my father would do if he found out.

"I will go," I said emphatically.

"Around two in the morning is the best time to go. I'll be outside your gate with the carriage. If you don't show up, I'll understand."

I heard movements in the foyer. It was my father who had arrived. Max appeared shortly afterward and asked Thomas to accompany him to Dr. Robert's office. We said our goodbyes, and I went upstairs to check out the news and the gifts my aunt had brought back from her trip.

Four

I was lucky that everyone at home would retire early to their rooms. Especially my father, who besides being a heavy sleeper, needed to be at the hospital at dawn to lecture or engage in some emergency surgery.

I descended the stairs to the hall, praying not to run into any servants wandering around the house. The servants' quarters were in the attic. No one would see me leave. The house was dimly lit. I opened the front door and left. Thomas's carriage was waiting for me.

"Rowena, you've lost your senses. You've just tarnished your reputation. No man will want to marry you now."

The night was cold, and a chill ran through my body. Before I could regret my reckless behavior, I ran, and opened the iron gate, which creaked as if chastising me for my stealthy departure.

I opened the carriage door and got in. The vehicle started moving, and I could relax. It was very cold that night, I wore a shawl over my shoulders for warmth. Thomas laid a blanket over my legs to keep me warm. This gesture made me feel more protected by his side.

"Do you think we're doing the right thing, Mr. Fawcett?"

"I don't know! I believe so. Did you have any trouble leaving?"

"Leaving wasn't that difficult, we just can't linger."

"Are you prepared to see the young girl's body?"

"I think so. I examined a corpse in a class with my father the other day."

The carriage stopped in front of St. Thomas Hospital. The streets around were deserted. The dense shadow of the night filled me with fear. Thomas led me to a small side door of the building, where the caretaker was waiting. He guided us through a long corridor, and we descended a cold stone staircase, where he accompanied us to the morgue.

Thomas gave the man a few shillings, who then left us alone with the body of the young girl. Her pale, bloodless body lay on a white table. The sweet smell of the cadaver pervaded the room, making my stomach churn. I approached and examined the cut site. Her carotid artery had been sliced. That's where all her blood had been drained from. But how?

We spent some time examining the body and speculating about who and why they committed the crime. When Thomas decided to turn her to one side, to look for other evidence. A birthmark on the right shoulder of the girl caught my attention. At first, I was in shock, and suddenly, a chill took over my entire being. The smell around me, the lost youth of the girl, and the mark on her back, made my legs go weak. I leaned on the edge of the table. She had a mark in the same place as mine.

"Rowena, are you alright?" Thomas asked anxiously.

"Yes, let's get out of here," I lied.

I walked briskly back the way we came, towards the door where the caretaker had received us. Thomas followed, not understanding anything. I opened the exit. The street was very dark. A huge hand pulled me out so violently that I nearly fell to the ground. Another figure grabbed Thomas by the arms and dragged us into a small alley. Thomas struggled to break free while I, with one hand free, threw punches at the chest of my captor, which had no effect. My punches were too weak to affect the brute overpowering me.

Thomas took a punch to the stomach, falling to his knees on the ground, doubled over in pain. Our attackers started talking nonsense. Something about us invading their territory to steal bodies, that they proclaimed themselves the owners. Even in that dark alley, I could feel the hatred emanating from those words.

We were going to die. We needed to escape. Still trapped, I lifted the heel of my boot as high as I could and brought it down with all my might, stomping on the foot of the man holding me. He screamed in pain, and for a moment, let me go. I elbowed him in the stomach and pushed him back. Writhing in pain and off balance, he fell to the ground.

I ran towards Thomas, who was starting to get up, and in the same motion, I pulled out one of the long metal pins I was using to hold my hat in my hair and stabbed it with all my strength into the face of Thomas's attacker. As he howled in pain, and the lunatic who had held me tried to get up, I grabbed Thomas by the arm.

"Run, Thomas!" I yelled, pulling my friend.

Thomas's attacker, still blinded by the pain I had inflicted, tried to grab me. His hand groped blindly in the air but only managed to clutch part of the shoulder of my dress, which tore, thus allowing me to break free from his grasp.

We escaped the alley, but in the confusion, we ended up running in the opposite direction of where our carriage was located. By the time we realized, there was no turning back. Our assailants had recovered and were now frantically chasing after us. I lifted my skirts - long skirts are a disaster when you need to run - and ran like mad.

"I must have been out of my mind to be in that place at that time."

We entered filthy and foul-smelling alleys, trying to shake off our pursuers, but they kept on our trail. I began to gasp for breath. Then a voice whispered from a narrow alley, hidden in the shadows of the night.

"This way, Thomas!"

It was a boy. Thomas pulled me into the alleyway, barely wide enough for us to walk through. We followed the boy, looking back to see our two chasers pass by the alley entrance without stopping. The dark street and the dark alley helped hide the spot where we entered.

We continued walking along the alley, which seemed more like a labyrinth. Various properties backed onto this passage. We passed by dog kennels, tool sheds, and other unfinished structures until we reached the main street, far from those repulsive individuals.

I was tired and sore. Besides my dirty dress with a torn shoulder, exposing part of my décolletage and back, now that the adrenaline had worn off, I felt exposed. Thomas noticed my embarrassment, took off his coat, and draped it over my shoulders. I noticed he glanced at the birthmark, the tree of life, on my right shoulder.

"Rowena, you have a mark similar to that on the young woman who was murdered," he said in astonishment.

"I saw. It might just be a coincidence," I replied, still panting. "Who is this boy who helped us? He called you by your name."

"This is Bob Little. He has a group of street boys who know every inch of London. They are always helping me."

Thomas handed the boy three shillings.

"Thank you, Bob."

"I was near the hospital when I saw that the 'Body snatchers' had gotten you. They are very dangerous. So, I followed the group until I could help you. This is Maze Pond Webb Street, a quieter road, you'll be safe. Thomas, miss, I'm off, until another time." Bob tipped his cap slightly and left.

"Body snatchers, what do you mean, Thomas? Did they mistake you for a competitor? Is this what you do for my father? Do you steal bodies?" I asked, furious.

"No! Of course not! I would never steal a body. I have authorization from the morgue to take unclaimed bodies to the medical school. They are used for students to dissect, study anatomy, and the cause of death."

We were having this discussion when I noticed a carriage passing near where we were. Even though the area was dimly lit, I managed to identify the emblem drawn on the vehicle's door. It was my family's.

"My father's carriage. What is he doing here and at this hour?" I asked, taken aback.

The vehicle was slowing down, a sign that it was about to stop. Could he have seen me?

I quickly pulled Thomas back to the entrance of the alley we had emerged from, and we watched as the carriage stopped a short distance away.

My father got out, looked up and down the poorly lit street. The way he was acting, it seemed like he was worried about being followed. He wasn't looking for us; he simply hadn't seen us. He climbed the steps to the house door, and rang the brass knocker three times. Some time later the door opened, and he went inside.

Right after the door closed, another carriage with its curtains drawn slowly passed by my father's vehicle. The carriage briefly stopped in front of the house and then left. My father was right. Someone was following him.

We stayed rooted to the spot for a while, anxious about Dr. Robert coming out soon. We were dirty and tired. Thomas felt cold because I was wearing his coat. My legs started to complain.

"Poor things, I had demanded too much of them tonight."

With great caution, we walked towards home. At that moment, a carriage approached us and the driver spoke:

"Mr. Fawcett. Please, get in." It was Thomas's coachman, who had found us.

The boy, Bob, after leaving us, had gone back to the hospital and informed the coachman where he could find us. He was small, but he was quite clever.

We passed in front of the house my father had entered. I did not recognize the house. It might have been a beautiful residence once, but time had been unkind to it, and now it was crying out for a renovation.

Five

I woke up late, and my body ached all over. I rang the bell, and Lucy showed up. I asked her to prepare my breakfast and that I would be down as soon as I was dressed. I handed her my dirty and torn dress to give to the laundress and, knowing Lucy was skilled at sewing, I asked her to mend it for me once it was clean. Of course, with as much secrecy as possible.

After breakfast, I headed to the library and was startled to find my father, reading the newspaper in his favorite armchair. Odd that he hadn't gone to the hospital. My sister was slumped in another armchair, needlework in hand, creating a beautiful floral embroidery. Was father waiting for me? Did he see us last night?

"Good morning, father. Hello, Emily. Aren't you heading to Barts today?"

"Only in the afternoon. I have no appointments this morning."

"Could you recommend a good book on arteries, especially the carotids? I'm conducting a study."

"Carotids? Odd. Have a look at that leather-bound volume," he pointed to a specific book in the library. "Handle it with care."

"Reading about arteries. Blood. How macabre," Emily commented, visibly disgusted.

I picked up the book he had recommended, and sat down, far from my sister. I needed to concentrate on my research, and Emily could distract anyone. I leafed through the book to the chapter that interested me, the carotids. I found a very suggestive illustration, showing the entire function of the artery, going from the neck to the aortic arch, which connects to the heart.

As I turned the next page, a folded paper fell onto my lap. I unfolded the yellowed sheet. It was a note from my father. I recognized his handwriting right away.

"If you make an eight-centimeter incision between the shoulder and neck, pull out the carotid artery, and insert a cannula - a long metal tube -, forcing the blood out by either aspiration or gravity. This is undoubtedly the best procedure for draining blood from the body."

So that was the method used to drain the blood from the body of the young woman who was murdered.

"My God, what a horror!"

Why had my father written this note and kept it?

Max entered the library and informed Dr. Robert that Inspector Tennyson was waiting for him in the sitting room. He left the newspaper on the couch and went to meet him in the office.

I folded the paper I was reading and placed it back on the same page I found it. I got up and arranged the book on the shelf. I needed to find out what information the inspector had brought. Could it be a new murder?

I walked to the office. Darn, it was closed. I couldn't just stand there with my ear pressed against the door, trying to eavesdrop. I might get caught. I knocked on the door and entered.

"Good morning, inspector. Excuse me, father. Would you like me to bring some coffee?"

"No need to trouble yourself, but tell Max to prepare something."

I went to speak to the butler, but did not close the door completely. I left a slight crack open. I notified Max and quickly went back, standing by the office next to where they were. My hand on the doorknob, I wanted to avoid any surprises. At any rate, I could pretend I was about to enter.

The inspector, with his commanding presence, spoke loudly. The gap I had left in the door allowed me to overhear them even though I was a bit away. They were discussing a new murder that had occurred earlier that morning. The young woman's body was found in an alley, off Maze Pond Webb.

"Good heavens! That's the street Thomas and I were on earlier this morning. My father was there, too."

Max appeared with a tray to serve them, bringing coffee and a bottle of brandy. He excused himself and entered. Upon leaving, he locked the door. My chance was lost; I couldn't overhear them anymore. The closed door muffled the sound of their voices; I would have to press my ear against it to hear anything. Despite my curiosity, I wasn't going to risk it.

I lingered for a few more moments in front of the office entrance, trying to digest what I had heard. A crime at the location we had been just hours before. I was so absorbed in thought that I didn't notice them leaving the cabinet. I quickly turned the doorknob, pretending that I was about to enter the office. My father bid farewell to the inspector and returned to his study. I went to his door, knocked gently, and entered.

"If you don't mind, daughter, I would like to be alone for a while."

"Bad news from the inspector?" I persisted, despite his apparent sadness.

"Another young woman dead. In the same manner as the other."

"Did you know her? You seem so sad!"

"Please, I would rather not discuss this matter with you right now."

"Yes, dad. I'm sorry."

He was so distressed, it seemed as if he knew the victim. Strange. I closed the door and went to my room. Perhaps Thomas, as a journalist, would know more details. I wrote him a note, setting a meeting at the Twinings tea house, to talk about the death of this young woman that had deeply affected my father.

I asked the cook's helper to deliver the letter to the address Thomas had given me, and to await his reply.

Thomas was waiting for me at the tea house, along with biscuits, cakes, meringues, gingerbread, and the delicious Earl Grey tea. Everything was tempting, including Mr. Thomas Fawcett. But my focus was elsewhere.

"I found your invitation curious. But then I thought, perhaps Miss Stein misses my company?" said Thomas, with a tinge of irony.

"Don't flatter yourself, Mr. Fawcett. I made my reasons for our meeting quite clear in my note."

"Alright, Rowena. What do you want to know?" He asked. He then signalled the waitress to serve us tea with biscuits.

"My father was near the scene of the crime yesterday. I'm worried."

"We were there too. The young woman was Jo Darville's daughter, an actress, who lives in the house Dr. Robert visited yesterday."

"My father knew both victims. What is the inspector thinking about this?"

"For now, nothing. He currently thinks they are serial killings. He just doesn't know the motive yet. The inspector is perplexed by the lack of blood at the scenes where the victims are found. He believes they were killed elsewhere."

"Why does he think the deaths are connected?"

"They were killed in the same way, also drained of blood, and have birthmarks in the same place."

"Did Jo Darville's daughter also have the mark?"

"Yes. In the same place as yours. Only, the marks are different."

The biscuit scratched my throat as I swallowed, and a shiver ran down my spine. Could the killer be targeting all young women with any kind of birthmark he found? But why?

Six

U pon arriving home, I found Aunt Annie enjoying afternoon tea with Emily.

"Look who's here. We missed you," said my sister sarcastically.

"I went to the dressmaker," I lied.

I sat down with them, not wanting to seem rude. We talked about life's trivialities. Emily was ecstatic because the topic was the ball at the Holyhead residence - the hospital director's. My father had asked Auntie to accompany us. He made it clear that he wanted his two daughters to attend the ball.

He knew about my aversion to ballrooms. The very thought of attending these balls when I would be introduced to London society sent shivers down my spine. That's why he stressed to my aunt that we both had to be there.

It was Dr. Henry Holyhead's birthday, a grand event where families of London's leading surgeons would likely be present. And my father didn't want to look bad in front of his colleague.

"Rowena, will Mr. Fawcett also be at the party?" asked Aunt Annie, with a sly smile.

"It seems he's on good terms with the host. He'll probably be invited."

"Great. Your first dance will be with me," said Emily, beaming.

"Emily! He would probably prefer to dance first with your sister, or perhaps with other young ladies," said my aunt patiently.

"Why? I'm the prettiest!"

"It's not about who's the prettiest. Your sister is older. And you know, etiquette dictates that she should be asked to dance first by the gentleman."

"Etiquette, etiquette. Let's see who he'll prefer to ask to dance," said Emily, sulking.

The day of the party had arrived. Emily was radiant that morning. Various dresses were scattered across her bed, asking for my opinion on which one she should wear that night. Honestly, they were all beautiful. Emily always had good taste in her clothing, choosing the finest fabrics and the trendiest colors. But her youthful fervor never left her satisfied, always searching in fashion magazines for a new style.

"Poor Dad, always frantic about the bills coming from the dressmaker."

I chose a light green dress for Emily; it accentuated her beautiful face and my sister's gorgeous eyes. It was a dress with a spring vibe that reflected Emily's mood when she wasn't angry, of course.

We went to the ball that evening, accompanied by Aunt Annie. She looked dazzling in her blue dress, which matched her honey-colored eyes. I wore a delicate wine dress that complemented my dark brown hair and my greyish-blue eyes.

Carriages kept arriving, carrying elegantly dressed women, flaunting the latest fashion trends. We ascended the beautiful marble staircase of the Holyhead residence and found the ballroom bustling. The chandelier lights sparkled on the jewels and dresses, bringing the flowers in their prints to life.

Emily quickly spotted Thomas, who was conversing with my father and our host. Thomas' youthfulness and beauty radiated throughout the room, felt through the chatter among the young ladies and the looks directed at him.

We approached my father, and introductions were made to our host and his wife, who was seated in a position that best alleviated her pains. Dr. Holyhead, tall with impeccable posture and in his prime, had a rectangular face and a well-defined jaw that emphasized his probing gaze when he greeted me. I felt momentarily embarrassed. He noticed and immediately gave me a slight smile, easing my slight discomfort.

He introduced us to Mr. George Holyhead, his son. He appeared to be two or three years older than Thomas, with the same physical build as his father and the same "nose in the air" as our host. His face was stern, and his eyes revealed a bitter soul. A proud young man of good standing, but exuding a deep pain within. He soon excused himself to join a select group of his friends.

We stepped away to let Thomas, my father, and the hosts continue their conversation. At that moment, Mrs. Gertie Holyhead called Aunt Annie over and introduced her to a gentleman who promptly asked her to dance, which she happily accepted.

I was captivated for a while by the way she danced with such grace. Twenty-eight years old, gorgeous, and well-dowered. Exceptionally intelligent and opinionated. She broke completely from the stereotype of women from our era, who married at a young age. Auntie was single because men always looked for women who were submissive, bending to their wishes and commands without any debate, for marriage. And she was not one to conform. It didn't bother her. She cherished her freedom, which allowed her to travel endlessly. She often mentioned hoping to meet her future husband on one of her exotic travels.

Daydreaming about Auntie, I was pulled back to reality when Miss Joanna Fawcett, Thomas's sister, introduced Emily to a young man, asking her for a dance. Emily hesitated to accept. She had it in her head that her first dance would be with Thomas. Who, incidentally, still standing, was chatting with my father. His constant shifting from foot to foot, seeking support, showed he was growing impatient. Whether the conversation was dragging or he was eyeing us, wanting to join, I couldn't tell.

The young man left to find another partner, as Emily had bluntly declined his offer. Thomas's sister and her friend moved away from us. Another young gentleman asked me for a dance. I didn't accept. I wasn't rude about it. Thomas's intent gaze filled me with a deep sense of longing. Oh, how I wished to dedicate my first dance of the evening to him! After my refusal, the gentleman asked Emily if she would consider him for the next song. She too promptly rejected him.

Thomas then approached, we chatted about trivial things, and he then invited me to join him in the dance floor center. Emily was livid. She had decided days ago that Thomas's first dance would be with her.

"Thomas Fawcett, aren't you going to dance with me?" asked Emily rather sharply.

"Of course, Miss Emily Duncan. The next dance is yours," he replied.

Thomas gently led me into the dance, and Emily stormed off towards the refreshments, fuming.

"I was waiting for your sister to accept someone else's invitation to a song so that I could invite you, thus avoiding this awkward situation. But she was turning everyone down."

"Since the first plans for this ball, Emily had fantasized that her first dance would be with you."

"Your sister is a beautiful girl, but very willful."

I noticed Emily marching determinedly towards us, holding a glass of punch in her hands. When she got close, she pretended to trip on something, which obviously wasn't there, and spilled the entire contents of the glass on me. Thomas tried to pull me away, to avoid a larger mess, but it was too late. My dress was drenched, stained, and ruined.

"Emily, look what you've done!" I cried out in desperation.

"Sorry, Rowena. It wasn't my intention. I tripped," she said, with a sardonic smile.

"Of course, you intended to. It was on purpose."

Angry, I pulled away from Thomas's arms and ran towards the exit door. Crying, I descended the steps of the Holyhead, passed through its gardens. I wanted to be far from the embarrassment Emily had caused me. Far from everything. Far from everyone. Especially from my sister.

Seven

Frustrated, I left the party alone, still shaken, and without realizing I was drifting away from the ball, I started walking along the dimly lit streets, their lights flickering uncertainly. I had no destination in mind, not knowing which direction I was headed. Gradually, my blood cooled, and I realized the folly of my actions. I could have stayed in the Holyheads' gardens. I heard a faint noise near me, looked back, and was startled by the trail of darkness I was leaving behind. Seeing no one, panic gripped me, my heart racing at the folly of wandering alone at night. Feeling that someone or something was following me, I quickened my pace out of fear it might be a thief or the murderer with two victims already. I did not want to be the third. Despite the cold night, fear-induced sweat trickled down my forehead. A hand clutched my arm tightly while the other covered my mouth; I tried to break free but was dragged towards a darker corner, feeling filthy mud beneath my feet. The more I struggled, the tighter the grip on my arm became, causing immense pain.

"Isn't it a bit late for a pretty girl like you to be walking the streets?" the assailant said. "Give me your purse and jewelry, or I will kill you."

He tightened his grip on my arm further, nearly breaking it, and the tip of his knife pricked my neck. The alcoholic breath of the bandit and the stench of the mud at my feet started making me nauseous. I had no chance of any reaction, not with that blade pressed against my skin. Fear took over, and I felt like I was going to die.

"How naive of me to leave the ball alone, but Emily always had a way of throwing me off balance emotionally. It was too late for regrets now."

"Don't you know, young lady, that a girl from a good family shouldn't be walking down dark streets, let alone alone?" the villain said.

"But she's not alone!" that familiar voice sounded like a relief to my ears.

Surprised, the assailant looked back, and Thomas abruptly pulled him, causing him to lose his balance, letting go of my arm and moving the blade away from my neck. As Thomas pulled the bandit, he punched him, throwing him to the ground. Thomas was tall and well-built, but he struggled to subdue the scoundrel; he lacked the street smarts and experience of street men. Soon after hitting the ground, the attacker quickly stood up, and in an unexpected move, stabbed my friend in the arm.

In that moment, in a crazy burst of strength, I swung my purse with all the violence I could muster at the bandit's face. Thomas, taking advantage of the assailant's brief daze, punched him hard in the nose, making him fall unconscious onto the muddy ground.

In the distance, we heard whistles, likely from guards coming to see who was fighting.

"Thomas, let's get out of here. I don't want to cause any embarrassment to my father. Those police will ask a lot of questions I don't want to answer."

"Rowena, the wound is bleeding a lot, the bandit cut deep into my arm."

I took my handkerchief and tied it around Thomas' wound, trying to staunch the bleeding a bit.

"Let's go to a well-lit street and catch a carriage to my house. We can treat your wound in my father's clinic."

We arrived safely at my residence, asking Thomas to be quiet. I didn't want to wake any servants, let alone Penny and Max, and I didn't know if my father had arrived. Fortunately, the house was silent.

"We can take a better look at your wound here in the clinic." I removed the blood-soaked handkerchief I had tied around Thomas' arm. "Wow, the cut is deep, and it's still bleeding a lot. Could it have hit an artery?"

"Rowena, what are we going to do? We need to call Dr. Robert. He's a doctor and will know what to do."

"No, Thomas, my father must never find out what happened to us tonight. He'll lose trust in me, and never let me out of the house again."

I knew that the only solution for healing Thomas's wound lay in the decision I was about to make, even if it meant revealing my secret to him.

Could I trust him? His dazzling green eyes throw me into turmoil. But could I place my faith in him? I've known Thomas for such a short time.

His wound kept bleeding, even with the new bandage I had put on, which quickly soaked through with blood. My father would have stitched the cut perfectly, but I still hadn't mastered suturing properly, risking leaving an ugly scar on his arm, or worse, it could get infected, turn gangrenous, and Thomas might lose his arm. My God, what a horrifying thought, just imagining that possibility sent shivers down my spine. My father could arrive at any moment. It was the last thing I needed. I had to do something.

In the heat of the moment, without hesitation, I grabbed a scalpel from my father's medical equipment and removed the dressing from his arm.

"Rowena Stein, why do you need that scalpel? I need you to close my wound, not open another one."

I looked into his wide and fearful eyes and said:

"Thomas, I am risking my future at this moment. I'm going to trust you with the secret of my life. It's a secret that only my father knows. You're about to find out, and I hope you keep it with you forever."

I ran the scalpel across my arm, a cut formed, and blood emerged.

"Have you lost your mind Rowena?"

I took Thomas's injured arm, let a few drops of my blood fall onto his wound, and quickly pressed his injury against my bleeding cut.

"Trust me, Thomas"

I held his injury against mine for a few seconds, and when I pulled away, my cut was nearly healed and Thomas's wound had stopped bleeding, beginning to heal.

Thomas looked at me in astonishment and jerked his arm away, not understanding what was happening.

"Rowena Stein, are you a witch?"

"Calm down Thomas, let me explain. Please don't judge me, just listen. Ever since I was little, whenever I got hurt, the wound would heal within seconds. So, my father explained that I have a very rare blood type, one that allows me to heal myself." Thomas's eyes widened in astonishment. "Of course, I'm not immortal, but my wounds regenerate very quickly, in a matter of seconds. I've never been bedridden. My father asked me to keep it a secret, so people wouldn't judge me or think I'm a freak, like how you're seeing me right now. No one knows this secret, only my father and now you. I'm entrusting you with my life, and I hope you won't share it with anyone. I trust you."

I bandaged Thomas's arm and explained that he should heal by the next day because my blood, when in contact with any other, passes on its healing properties.

"Thomas, you need to go home now, before my father arrives. We're filthy, stinking, and covered in blood. And I need to clean up this mess, take a good bath, and rest."

"But Rowena..."

"Please Thomas..."

Of course, if my father found us alone and in that dreadful state, especially with Mr. Fawcett injured, it would be a scandal. Reluctantly, Thomas understood the situation and left.

In my room, after a warm and comforting bath, I started to ponder the events of that night. The recklessness of my action wandering around at night, knowing that a killer was on the loose. Was the man who attacked me the sought-after murderer, or just an opportunistic thief?

And would Thomas keep my secret? What if he was the murderer? Could I be his next victim?

I eventually fell asleep.

Eight

I woke up the next morning with Mary Penny drawing the curtains of my bedroom window, as she had brought my breakfast.

"Miss Stein, Dr. Robert is waiting for you in his office, right after you have breakfast," Penny said.

I hurried through my breakfast; my father must have been eager for an explanation about the events of the previous night. I went downstairs and knocked on the office door, asking for permission to enter. I found my father sitting in his comfortable leather armchair, behind his mahogany desk, and my sister leaning on a sofa.

"Good morning, Rowena Duncan Stein, could you explain to me what happened last night that made you leave the ball and run off into the night on your own? It caused the whole of London society present at the ball to speak ill of you. Not to mention, your behavior was disrespectful towards our host, Dr. Henry Holyhead."

When my father used my full name, it was a sign he was very angry and would not tolerate any excuses.

"I'm sorry, Papa. Emily always manages to get under my skin. She deliberately spilled a glass of punch on my dress, ruining it, just because Mr. Thomas Fawcett chose to dance with me instead of her."

"That's a lie; it was an accident!" Emily shouted.

"Emily, watch your tone," my father said.

"It doesn't matter, Rowena. You could have just apologized to our host and asked your aunt to accompany you home. Not run off from the party into the night on your own like you lost your senses, especially with a murderer on the loose in the streets of London."

"Sorry, I got upset by what Emily did, and before I knew it, I was walking alone through the streets, but Mr. Fawcett followed me and brought me safely home in a rented carriage."

"Another mistake, Rowena. You know it's not proper for a young lady in our society to be out at night alone with a man who is neither her father nor her husband."

"I know, Papa," I said, lowering my head.

"I also heard that two guards arrested a potential thief, half-conscious, carrying a knife. He was found on a street in the direction you took. You and Thomas had nothing to do with this, I hope."

I could never tell my father what happened with me and Thomas. I would be severely reprimanded, and he would lose all his trust in me.

"Of course not, Papa. Imagine me and Mr. Fawcett facing off against a criminal. That would be quite the spectacle. He just put me in a rented carriage and accompanied me back here. I didn't want to return to the ball because of the incident with my dress."

"About that incident with your dress, I've spoken to your sister, and she promised it won't happen again."

My sister lowered her head, but I caught a glimpse of a sly smile on her lips. The talk Papa had with Emily, I believe, would do nothing to change her attitude towards me.

"I don't want, and I don't find it appropriate for you to be walking alone in the streets; it's not becoming of a young lady like you. The streets are full of predators, like this killer who is taking the lives of young ladies."

"Yes, Papa, it won't happen again," I said.

I left my father's office and went to my room. I felt like pulling my sister's hair out. She was such a hypocrite. I got a lecture from my father, and Thomas was seriously injured because of her childish behavior, not to mention I could have been killed at the hands of that robber. I wrote a message for Thomas, folded the paper, and sealed it with my wax seal.

I needed to know how his wound was and ask him to accompany me on a visit to a certain lady.

I called for Max, who informed me that Dr. Robert had gone to the hospital, so I handed him the message, asking him to deliver it to Mr. Fawcett as quickly as possible.

"But Miss Stein, this young man is a journalist, your father wouldn't approve of you associating with him."

"Max, Max, he's just a friend, and a friend of your employer. Besides, Papa doesn't need to know anything about this note. You agree, Max?"

"Yes, Miss," Max said reluctantly.

I couldn't use any of our family's carriages; they bore the family crest on their doors. I wouldn't want anyone finding out about my surreptitious departure. A bit later, I walked to the nearest taxi stand, took a rented carriage, and went to the place I had arranged to meet Thomas. It was the street where, a few nights ago, we saw my father entering a suspicious house. Thomas, ever the gentleman, arrived on time.

"Rowena Stein, what are we doing here where there was a murder?" Thomas inquired anxiously.

"Visiting a likely friend of my father."

I asked Thomas to look at the wound on his arm. He hesitated, because since leaving the office last night, he hadn't removed the bandage I had applied, fearing the wound might start bleeding again. He took off his coat, rolled up his shirt sleeve, and removed the bandage covering the cut, showing me his arm. Where there had been an open stab wound the night before. Now, at that moment, there was only a reddish mark on his skin, which would soon disappear. Even I was impressed by Thomas's swift healing.

"That's great, Thomas, your arm is healed."

Holding my hand in his, he began to stroke it, and with a mischievous smile said, "You have magical hands, my dear Rowena."

I felt the warmth emanating from his hands, even though I was wearing gloves. My cheeks began to blush slightly, and I quickly withdrew my hand, not wanting him to notice that I enjoyed his caress.

"Rowena Stein, is it me or are you blushing simply from my touch?" Thomas said, his eyes half-closed.

"Thomas! This is neither the time nor the place for such insolence. We are here on a very serious matter."

I explained to Thomas the reason we were standing in front of the house my father had visited. As a journalist and me posing as his assistant, we were planning to suggest to actress Jo Darville, the house's occupant, a feature article about her glory days in theater.

Thomas had told me he had gathered some information about her, on the day of her daughter's murder. Mrs. Darville was showing some signs of madness. Maybe we wouldn't get anything concrete about Dr. Robert. But I had to try.

Thomas knocked on the door knocker, and we waited for someone to open. A woman opened the door. My friend and I exchanged glances; she appeared to be in her thirties, had beautiful features, and elegant hair. She did not seem mad, as we had thought.

"What do you wish?" she asked with suspicion.

"My name is Thomas Fawcett and this lady is my assistant. We're from The Express. We're compiling a special feature on some actresses and have been sent to write an article about your artistic life. You didn't receive our letter?" Thomas lied.

"No, I believe not. But please, come in"—a smile lit up her face.

Her living room was small, sparingly furnished, but everything was perfectly placed. On the walls, there were paintings, photographs, and posters of her plays. The entire setup gave the room a cozy harmony.

We sat where indicated. She apologized for not having a servant as she prepared some tea. She returned with the tray and served us. Gradually, she began sharing her journey as an actress, the actors she had worked with, and the misfortunes of her profession. I could tell by the way her hands moved that she was starting to get agitated.

"You are young. Why did you stop acting?" Thomas inquired.

"Three years ago, I lost a great love. My world fell apart. I decided to stop acting for a while as I recovered emotionally. I thought about returning, but just couldn't. Now, I live on medications."

"Was he also an actor, your husband?" I asked curiously.

"Husband, no. He was my lover. My husband, he passed away some time ago"—she smiled. "Regis was a doctor. After his death, his friend Dr. Robert has been offering me financial support and taking care of my ailments."

"Forgive me. Is Dr. Robert your new lover?" I asked apprehensively, dreading her answer.

She burst into a mad laughter.

"No, dear. The two were friends from the time they studied and practiced medicine in Ingolstadt, southern Germany. In fact, Regis helped him bring over a baby, whom Robert had saved. Regis told me that his friend ended up adopting her as his daughter."

A black cloud passed over my eyes, an emptiness formed in my head, I felt like I was about to faint. My hands turned cold. My whole body felt weak. I leaned on the arm of the chair and took a deep breath. Asking,

"Baby?"

"Never mind. I've spoken too much," she said nervously.

She started to cry, blaming herself for her daughter's recent death. That night she was in the midst of an episode of her illness, and her nervous daughter had gone out seeking Dr. Robert's help—my father—and she never returned.

In shock, I paid no further attention to what she was saying. I bid the woman, who was still crying, farewell. Thomas and I left. Outside, a whirlwind of thoughts raced through my mind. All I wanted was to go home.

Nine

I bid Thomas farewell. He insisted on accompanying me, given my fragile state. However, I wanted and needed to be alone, to ponder everything the actress had shared with us. Especially when she revealed that my father had an adopted daughter, that had shocked me. I needed to find out who this person was. Was it me? Was it Emily? Emily couldn't be the one, as we had a painting of her as a baby at home. Thomas flagged down a rental carriage and instructed the coachman on where to take me. I was still stunned by all I had heard.

Upon arriving home, I went straight to my father's study. I rarely entered there as he didn't allow anyone in his office without him being present, not even me. I knew at that moment, he would be teaching classes at the medical school of the hospital. I took a gamble on a minor invasion of his privacy, luckily the door wasn't locked – probably our housekeeper had forgotten to lock it after one of the maids cleaned the room.

I entered, closed the door behind me, and tried to be as discreet as possible to avoid making noise. I needed to find any evidence of the adoption Mrs. Darville had told me about. I started with the bookshelves, checking if there were any documents tucked between the volumes. Nothing. Of course, naive of me, such an important document wouldn't be in easy reach. It must be hidden away somewhere secret. Yet, I needed to find it. I searched the cabinets, sifting through all the papers I came across. Found nothing. I went on to search through a few unlocked drawers on his desk, rifling through agendas. I opened folders. I was opening the last drawer when I heard a noise from the vestibule, someone had just arrived. I rushed and positioned myself near the door, recognizing my father's voice. Foolish me, in my search, I hadn't noticed the hours passing by. And now? If my father found me there, in his study, I would be in deep trouble.

I heard his footsteps approaching, and the door next to mine opening and closing, he went into the office. I needed to get out of there as quickly as possible, remembering the semi-open drawer when I heard the noise in the vestibule. I rushed back to the desk and in my hurry slammed the drawer shut with considerable force. A small bundle of letters and newspaper clippings, tied with a ribbon, fell to the floor. It must have been attached to the bottom of the drawer, or in some secret compartment that opened.

Eager to know the contents, I picked up the bundle and quickly untied the ribbon. There were old newspaper clippings, letters, and notes from my father. The first clipping caught my attention immediately; it was dated 1831, the year of my birth. It spoke of a fire in a small village in southern Germany, where all the newborn babies had disappeared. And mentioned that the villagers, at the time, still did not know whether these children had been killed in the fire or kidnapped by invaders who had set the village ablaze.

My legs started to feel incredibly weak, I leaned my back against the wall and slowly slid to the ground, sitting on my dress. I forgot where I was. I spread all the clippings, letters, and notes around me and began to cry. My father had told me he had been a doctor in a village in Germany. Hence my nightmares of fleeing from a burning town.

"My God! I'm adopted."

The office door opened, my father came in and shut the door behind him, and I continued to cry, still sitting on the floor, too weak to go through the rest of the documents I had found.

"Oh, my dear! This is not how I wanted you to find out," my father said almost whispering.

He bent down, hugged me, took one of my hands and led me to the nearest armchair, where I sat down. Then he knelt at my feet and said:

"You are British because you were registered here in London, but you were born in a small village near Constance, in southern Germany." My father took a handkerchief from his coat pocket and gently wiped away my tears streaming down my face. "You remember those nightmares about a village catching fire, that you always have? It was right after I had delivered you. Your mother was a beautiful villager, but blind from birth. One day during your escape, the wounded Frankenstein's monster appeared in the village, and without anyone noticing, hid in your mother's cabin, which was the most secluded of all. She, unaware that he was a monster, took care of his apparent wounds by touch. The few guttural words expressed by the monster, touched her heart, for they were laments of agony, the same anguish she felt for being blind. She cared for him affectionately for days, and the creature, touched by her kindness, calmed down, and they gave themselves to each other. Your mother told me it was a magical moment in her life. She was very lonely, and even without knowing he was a monster, felt that he truly loved her in that moment."

"No! I am the daughter of a monster!"

My father sat next to me, tenderly placing my head on his lap, and continued:

"No, Frankenstein wasn't a monster; he was a tormented being. He ran away from his creator because he desperately wanted a companion, and Dr. Victor, his creator, denied him that. The world saw him as a monster and hunted him down. In the village where he was hiding, being looked after by his mother, when the villagers discovered him, they attacked the monster, thinking he was terrorizing his mother. So, the creature fled, leaving her pregnant with you."

"How do you know all these details?" I said, sobbing.

"I was the village doctor; I used to visit them once a month to bring medicine and treat the sick. And your mother was my patient; I took care of her throughout her pregnancy. She had a difficult labor; the villagers thought she was going to give birth to a monster. On the day you were born, the village was stormed and set on fire, looking for Frankenstein's daughter who had just been born. I fled with you and your mother, entering the forest surrounding the village, and from a distance, we watched it burn."

"Why did they want to kill me? Did they think I was a monster like my father too?" I said with a sob.

"Your mother was beautiful, and you greatly resemble her; that wasn't the reason. It was because of the healing properties in your blood," said my father, stroking my hair.

"But how did they know? I had just been born," I said, wiping my tears.

"In correspondence with my friend Dr. Victor, he wrote mentioning that if the creature had any offspring, the blood of that person would have some rare property. They must have been tracking the creature for months and heard some villager talking about the birth of a child whose father was the monster. That's what I deduced from reading those letters and documents I also exchanged with other colleagues back then."

"Does my sister know about this story?"

"No, nobody knows you're adopted, not even your sister, nor Mary Penny, and especially not Max. To everyone, your mother is Charity, the same as Emily's, who died giving birth. Your real mother is also deceased. She died a few months after your birth, from typhoid fever. I couldn't save her. The important thing is you know that I am your real father. I'm the one who raised you, with love and care."

My father gathered all the newspaper clippings and letters I had spread on the floor, tied them with a ribbon, and advised me to read everything in my room, with the door locked. There, as he said, I would find more details about my birth.

Someone knocked on the door; my father turned the key and opened it. It was Max.

"Dr. Henry Holyhead is waiting for you in the living room," said Max.

"Max, bring him here. Daughter, we'll continue our talk later."

I asked permission from my father and went up to my room. I locked the door because I needed to read all those documents calmly. I cried for a long time, distressed by what I had discovered. I spread the pieces of newspapers and letters on the bed, and noticed that one of the clippings was missing, the first one that caught my attention, about the fire in the village on the day of my birth. Darn, did it stay in my father's study?

"Did it fall without me noticing?"

I got up and searched the floor of my room, under the furniture, and especially under the bed, because the movement of my dress might have thrown it underneath. Nothing.

I resigned myself to having lost it. Then, there was a knock at the door. I opened just a crack; it was my father. He entered and closed the door behind him. In his hand, he held the clipping, which I thought I had lost. His expression was one of concern. He extended his hand and gave me the small piece of newspaper.

"Why do you look so worried, Dad?"

"Dr. Holyhead found the clipping on the floor of the study and asked a million questions. He showed more interest than usual, maybe because he knew I had been the doctor of that village."

"Does he know I am the monster's daughter?" I asked anxiously.

"No, under no circumstances. He doesn't even know you are adopted. Perhaps his interest is only because both of us were friends of Dr. Victor, the creature's father."

"Do you think he suspects something about my birth?"

"No, stay calm. I believe I managed to satisfy Holyhead's curiosity," Dad held my hands and asked. "One doubt is haunting me, who told you that you are adopted?"

At that exact moment, someone knocked on my room door.

"Yes!" said my father.

"Excuse me, doctor, Mr. Fawcett is waiting for you downstairs in the living room. He needs to speak with you urgently."

"I'm coming down, Max."

"Whew! Saved by the bell."

Ten

I hastily gathered all the scattered papers on the bed, taped them up any old way, and stored the bundle in my desk, locked it with a key, and ran after my father, managing to catch him as he was descending the stairs.

My sister was entertaining Thomas, trying as always to wrap him around her finger with her charm. Upon seeing us, Thomas rose, greeted my father and me, and said:

"I beg your pardon, Dr. Robert! Another young woman has been murdered."

"How did you find out, Thomas?" my father said apprehensively.

"I've just been with Inspector Tennyson, and he told the newspapers that the girl was found early this morning, near Regent's Canal in Pentonville, with a birthmark similar to the other victims' and a cut on her throat. But this time, they didn't drain her blood."

"Why not?" I asked.

"The inspector believes someone witnessed the crime scene, so the murderer fled for fear of being caught."

"How dreadful, I need your protection, Mr. Fawcett. - said my sister with a dose of sarcasm."

Honestly, my sister has a way of getting on my nerves. I looked at Thomas, and he gave me a knowing half-smile, aware of how Emily's antics bothered me. I excused myself to my father and headed to the garden.

"Emily, go upstairs! Thomas and I need to continue our conversation in the library, without interruptions."

I was sitting on my favorite bench when Thomas appeared in the garden after a while. He didn't even dare mention Emily's flights of fancy. He excused himself and sat down beside me.

"I didn't mention to Dr. Robert the name of the mother of this young woman who was killed. I didn't want to worry him."

"Why? Did my father know her?"

"The inspector informed me that she had worked here in your house."

"Here? When?"

"Mrs. Becky was a young kitchen helper."

"She worked here? I don't remember her."

"It was before your sister was born. You were very young. The inspector mentioned she got pregnant back then, and the cook asked for her resignation."

"She was pregnant with the girl who was murdered?"

"It seems so."

"What a sad fate! Lost her job for being pregnant with a girl, whose life was also taken."

"The odd thing is that all the victims had some connection to your father."

"What are you suggesting? That my father is the murderer?"

"Of course not! These facts are merely coincidences. Dr. Robert, a murderer? That would be the last straw."

"Do the police think the same?"

"The inspector knows that the deaths aren't random. Because the criminal is killing girls with the same characteristics."

"Would you like to visit the mortuary with me tonight, to see this mark, and examine what it has in common with yours? Perhaps you'll discover a clue by examining the body."

"No Thomas, on our last visit, we were attacked by those insane body snatchers."

"I agree Rowena, but they caught us off guard. Tonight, I'll be prepared. Besides, I'll be in a different carriage, without the family crest, and my coachman will be there for our safety. He's quite a sturdy man."

Despite being scared, I agreed with Thomas, his tone of voice gave me confidence. I was intrigued because girls around my age were dying, and all of them had birthmarks. I didn't believe in coincidences.

Late at night, I crept down the stairs quietly and unnoticed, went out through the garden, wearing a black velvet dress to better blend into the shadows of the night. Thomas waited for me in his cabriolet right in front of my gate, his driver helped me up. Thomas was right, his coachman was indeed a sturdy man. I felt more at ease.

I sat beside Thomas since his carriage had only two seats and was open at the front.

"You could have come with a closed carriage, it's cold tonight."

"This car is much faster. As for the cold, the warmth of our bodies will keep us warm. Besides, you look very beautiful in that dress."

"Thomas Fawcett, you never miss a moment to woo me. It was foolish of me to come. Stop, I want to get off."

"No Rowena, please forgive me. Stay, I'll behave."

Thomas moved further to his corner, draped a blanket over my legs, and we continued our journey.

That night, the moon was high in the sky, and the silhouettes of trees and buildings were highlighted by its light. We arrived at St. Thomas Hospital, located south of the Thames River, where the silence was deafening. Thomas asked Wilkes, his coachman, to stop in front of the main entrance and to be on the lookout in case we needed his help.

We went to a small side door of the hospital. Thomas, having been there that afternoon, had arranged with the caretaker, who was waiting for us. We entered the building cautiously, not wanting to bump into any body snatchers. The caretaker pointed us in the direction we already knew and left. We descended the cold stone staircase to the morgue, where the young woman's body awaited us on a table.

"My God! She was so young."

Thomas gently turned her body to the side, and I saw the mark. It wasn't like mine, but it was on the same shoulder. Looking at her hand, something glittered on her fingers. Could it be a ring?

I took her hand, opened her fingers, and pulled out the object wedged between them. No, it wasn't a ring. It was a silver cufflink with an embedded stone. A shiver ran through me, feeling as though someone was watching us, I started to panic, fearing I might be the next victim.

"Let's leave, someone is watching us," I whispered to Thomas.

"Relax. It's probably the caretaker," he replied.

We started walking back the way we came and heard footsteps ascending the staircase. We climbed the steps quickly, just in time to see the back door opening and a shadow that appeared to be a well-dressed man leaving through it. The sound of the door closing echoed down the corridor.

We ran to our cabriolet, and Thomas told Wilkes to follow the carriage that had just left. The other vehicle had a good head start on us.

"Faster," yelled Thomas. "We have to catch up."

Our coachman pushed the horse, and we quickly began to close the distance. Thomas didn't want to lose sight of it; we needed to know where it was going and who was in that carriage.

Probably, the intruder was in the morgue looking for the cufflink I had found on the dead girl's hand. But our arrival thwarted his search. Could he be the murderer? We were mad, in the dead of night, chasing a serial killer the police were after.

We continued following the carriage for some time, but I believe our fugitive realized he was being followed because his vehicle started to pull away again.

"Mr. Fawcett, they've increased the carriage's speed, I believe they've noticed we're on their tail," our driver said.

"Then do the same, make our horse run faster," Thomas said, nervously.

Our cabriolet sped up, and I began to feel the unevenness of the cobblestones beneath our vehicle. The cold wind whipped our faces, as our carriage was open at the front. I feared for our safety; I had never been in a carriage at this speed. My heart felt like it was about to leap out of my chest. We started to close the distance as our cabriolet was much lighter and faster than the fugitive's carriage.

Thomas, with his eyes squinted against the wind lashing our faces, yelled in desperation, barely able to discern the vehicle we were pursuing in the darkness of the night.

I became nervous, with every pothole our carriage jumped and hit the ground hard, seeming like it would fall apart. The horse was becoming exhausted from the speed and effort we were demanding of it.

I sensed we entered a downhill stretch, and further ahead, the road took a sharp turn. Continuing at this speed, our carriage would surely overturn, shatter, and we could die.

"Stop! Stop!" I screamed in desperation.

Thomas looked at me, startled, and I pointed desperately at the curve ahead. Thomas leaned out the side of the carriage and yelled:

"Stop, Wilkes! Stop now!"

The coachman seemed dazed, caught up in the frenzy of the chase, and hadn't seen the curve approaching. Thomas' screams snapped him out of his trance, and he pulled on the reins, slowing the animal. We managed to navigate the curve safely. But it was too late, the other carriage, being larger and more stable, was far away. We couldn't catch up anymore.

I looked at the cufflink in my hand, and a thought troubled me.

"Was this what the fugitive was looking for when he encountered us? Could he be the killer of those poor girls?"

Eleven

That night, I found it difficult to fall asleep. The thrill of the chase and the memories of the conversation I had with my father brought on an anguish in my chest. I was the daughter of a monster, even though my mother didn't feel that way, but that did not lessen the fact. Tears streamed down my cheeks; I wiped them away, I had to be strong. My real father was Robert Duncan Stein, a doctor and professor, the man who raised me, gave me affection and love. That was the truth. Thoughts still pounded in my head, but worn out, I eventually fell asleep.

I woke up with a start, having dreamt of gloved hands tightening around my neck, the wrists adorned with cufflinks inlaid with emeralds, just like the one in my possession. Lucy had entered my room and was opening the curtains.

"Miss Stein, Mr. Thomas Fawcett is downstairs and would like to speak with you," she said, seeing me wake up.

"Ask him to wait in the living room; I'll get dressed and be right down."

I was curious about why Thomas had sought me out so early in the morning. As I descended, I witnessed a rather pathetic scene. My sister Emily was keeping Thomas company, clearly making him uncomfortable with her insinuations and jokes, which were unbecoming for a lady of her age. She was bent on winning him over at any cost, and the way she was going about it seemed vulgar to me. It was a good thing father wasn't home; he would certainly have given her a stern punishment.

Thomas quickly stood up, upon seeing me descend the stairs, his face showing a relief that I had arrived.

"You could have taken a bit longer to get ready," my sister said mockingly. "We were having such a delightful conversation."

"Thomas, could we go to the garden to talk?" I asked.

"Why don't we all stay here and continue our conversation. What do you think of that idea, Mr. Thomas?" said Emily with a sly grin.

"Thank you for the invitation Miss Emily Duncan, but I need to discuss an urgent matter with Miss Stein."

"Secrets? How intriguing. Let father know about this," Emily said mockingly, as she ascended the stairs to her room.

I walked to the bench in our garden, and Thomas followed me, never once mentioning my sister's behavior, which he knew deeply upset me.

"Thomas, what brings you here so early? Did something happen?"

"I was missing your beautiful eyes, Rowena."

I blushed; I wasn't expecting such a straightforward response. Thomas had always flirted with me, but never so openly.

"Please, Mr. Thomas Fawcett! I believe you didn't come here just to pay me compliments."

"Forgive me, Rowena, but the emotions and dangers of last night's chase made me think a lot about you. About us. Moreover, there's been a new development."

"What? A new victim?" I asked apprehensively.

"No, after our visit to the morgue, someone stole the girl's body."

"How? Why?"

"I believe the theft of the body is related to the cufflink you found; it must be quite incriminating for the murderer," Thomas said. "Since we foiled his intentions yesterday, he decided to steal the corpse."

"He didn't know we found it," I said.

"Yes, that's why we are in danger," he said with concern.

"Just as we don't know his identity, he doesn't know who we are," I said, though not very convinced.

"Not yet, but judging by his clothes and carriage, he's a man of means. Therefore, he won't spare any effort to find us," Thomas said.

"I agree with you, but we have the upper hand. We have this." I opened my hand and showed him the cufflink I'd found on the young woman's fingers.

Thomas took it from my hand and began to examine it. The glint of the small emerald embedded in its surface caught my eye. He was right; this jewel belonged to a wealthy man.

"I have a feeling I've seen a cufflink with this same decoration. I just can't remember where or with whom," I said.

Thomas asked to keep the jewel. He would search with his artisan friends, who worked with precious stones, for any clues.

I bade him farewell and left him free to conduct his search. I went up to my room. I entered and locked the door, as I needed some privacy to review the contents of the package I had found in my father's study.

Since the night before, a premonition had been screaming in my mind. Could the deaths of the young women be linked to my birth? All three victims were about my age and bore birthmarks similar to mine, and they had some connection to my father; this couldn't be a mere coincidence. I took the package that my father had returned to me and which I hadn't yet had time to examine more closely. I removed the ribbon that tied it and spread everything on the bed: the letters and newspaper clippings. I didn't know what I was looking for, but I was going to read line by line those documents and articles mentioning the town, my mother, and the creature, until I found something.

After some time, two things caught my attention: a letter and a newspaper clipping. The letter was from Dr. Victor, in response to one from my father. In it, the doctor narrated that he had a diary where he had noted the entire process used in the creation of the monster, but he was concerned because this book had been stolen from his lab. He also mentioned that the creature's dream was to have a companion, as it felt lonely and wanted to start a family, which Dr. Victor had disagreed with. Moreover, he commented in his letter that, according to his research documented in the stolen diary, the creature's descendant would have some special gene, likely in the blood, due to the way it was created and the high electric charge the monster had been exposed to in order to create life.

I set the letter down and placed it on the bed. Now I understood why I was born with special, rare blood. Then I picked up the newspaper clipping, which had also caught my attention, and read it again. It mentioned the birth of a girl, daughter of a blind villager and the creature, and this child had a birthmark on her back, right at the shoulder level. On that day, an armed group following clues left by the creature, arrived at the village and discovered the birth of the monster's daughter. Since they couldn't find the child the villagers talked about, they set fire to the village in anger.

"My God, not only am I the daughter of the monster, but I'm also guilty for being the reason my village was wiped out."

However, Dr. Robert Duncan had fled with me and my mother as soon as the group arrived at the village. Sixteen years later, someone discovered that this baby, now a young woman, was living in London, and they were after her. I was the prey. A chill ran through my entire being; he wanted my blood. That's why they were draining the blood of those poor girls, who they believed were me. Anxiously, I stowed the clippings, well hidden in my desk.

I needed to talk to Thomas about all this. But how? Without revealing to him that I was the daughter of a monster.

I was descending the stairs to the library when our cook, Mrs. Butler, anxiously intercepted me. I found her behavior strange; we usually talked in the kitchen.

The matters related to our house; maintenance, employee payments, and food costs, were managed by my father. And I took care of the organization of the home and the employees. The domestic affairs in our house were beginning to cause me problems ever since the housekeeper Mary Penny started working with us, just over a year ago. There has always been some rivalry between her and Mrs. Butler, who, besides being older and having been with us longer, did not take orders from Penny. The two were always at loggerheads with each other. Both had their autonomy with their assistants. But it was Mary Penny's job to supervise and keep our house well-stocked.

I never took those squabbles seriously, as they didn't hamper the smooth running of the household.

"What's the matter, Mrs. Butler? You seem agitated."

"Some food items are missing from our pantry."

"Talk to Penny. She will handle it."

"Miss Stein. I informed her about the issue, and she accused me of wasting food, which is why it's missing. And me, of all people, who is so frugal."

"Calm down, Mrs. Butler. You've been with us for a long time. There's no better cook than you," I tried to soothe her. "What food do you think has gone missing?"

"Cooked ham, seed cake, chunks of butter, eggs, and tea."

"Did they all disappear at once?" I asked, shocked.

"No. A little at a time, over these last two weeks. I only noticed when I needed them for preparing a dish. Surely, I would remember if I had used them."

I reassured Mrs. Butler, promising to give her complaints special attention. Our staff had always been trustworthy, and there had never been complaints about our cook with anything disappearing in the kitchen. Especially because they considered Mrs. Butler a second mother. She always let them have seconds of any dish they liked. This disappearance of food was strange. I would be more vigilant.

I also needed to pay more attention to Mary Penny's unscheduled departures on her days off. She was leaving without my permission, but why? I had alerted Max to notify me the next time the governess made an unscheduled exit.

Twelve

I woke up to Lucy informing me that Thomas was waiting for me in the living room, that Dr. Robert had gone to the hospital, and Emily was at the seamstress's.

Lucy helped me with my attire. I put on a light green silk dress that made me look more radiant. I needed to feel beautiful and chase away the sadness I was feeling.

I went downstairs, and Thomas came towards me, helping me down the last few steps. He offered a charming smile, bringing his lips to my hand.

"You look beautiful, Rowena!" he said sincerely and affectionately.

A shiver ran up my body to my face; it wasn't proper for a young lady like me to have such sensations, but Thomas knew how to make me blush.

"Thank you, Mr. Fawcett. What brings you here so early?" I said as sternly as possible, to give myself time to recover.

"I wanted to fall into his arms and kiss him".

"Why do you play hard to get when I know you actually want to fall into my arms?" he questioned with a smile and half-closed eyes.

"Please Thomas, don't be cruel or insolent. I know you can't read minds."

"So, it's true. You were thinking about embracing me, and perhaps even kissing me. You've just admitted it."

"Thomas Fawcett, that's not what I said. What I meant was that since you can't read minds, you couldn't possibly know what I was thinking." My cheeks were burning with shame, surely very red.

Just then, Penny entered the room, excused herself, and announced that my breakfast was ready. Saving me from the embarrassment I was experiencing with Thomas. I invited him to join me for breakfast as we chatted.

Penny served us toast, butter, jams, and freshly brewed tea. Thomas, though he had already had his breakfast, nibbled a bit here and there, while catching me up on the latest news.

"Did you find out anything?" I asked as we sat down for breakfast.

"Yes, I visited some artisan friends and they referred me to two brothers who work exclusively with these types of cufflinks, featuring gemstone inlays. I believe they crafted this piece," Thomas said, handing me back the cufflink I had lent him. "Rowena, I would like you to accompany me to visit these two brothers after breakfast."

"Of course, I'll go. I want to find out who owns this object, I need to unearth some clue about the killer of these young women."

Thomas helped me into the carriage, sitting beside me. He had a look of concern on his face. Something was bothering him; I noticed the difference from the moment we left the breakfast table. I was also anxious, how to tell him that it was my blood the murderer was after. A slight jolt from the carriage, caused by a rock on the road, snapped us out of that trance.

"All three victims had birthmarks and were about your age. What is this killer looking for?"

"I believe someone knows that there's a girl with a birthmark on her shoulder, who possesses rare, healing blood. And they're trying to find that young woman," I said cautiously.

"But how would he know about the power of your blood if you've never mentioned this fact to anyone."

"I don't know, but someone is familiar with the properties of blood. We need to find out who it is, and why they need it, because they'll kill more youths before they get to me. And when they do find me, they'll kill me as well."

Thomas took my hand, placed it between his, and squeezed it tightly. Fear was clear in his gaze and in his gesture. I didn't pull my hand away, I was frightened too, and feeling very alone. I was in a real bind, I couldn't tell my father what was happening, let alone Emily. She would shun me even more if she knew I was adopted, especially being a descendant of a monster. Thomas knew about the blood but I would never tell him about the adoption, he couldn't even imagine that I was Frankenstein's daughter. It was obvious he would despise me. What good was having blood with such magic if you were hunted down like an animal, like an aberration. Nobody caring whether you were a living being, with feelings, desires, fears, and frustrations.

"My God, what torment"

Instinctively, I squeezed Thomas's hand. He looked at me and smiled mischievously. He was getting it all wrong. So, I gently removed my hand and placed it on my lap.

The rental carriage took us to Hatton Garden, where the most respected jewelry artisans in London were located. The cab stopped in front of a small two-story building, which boasted the sign Shreeve & Stephens. Thomas helped me out, paid the coachman, and dismissed him.

We stood at the door of the establishment, looking for someone who could give us information. Near the reception, there was a glass-enclosed office with two men inside, the taller, slimmer gentleman stood up and approached us.

"Good morning! I'm Mr. Stephens, how may I assist you?"

"Pleasure, I'm Mr. Fawcett and this is my assistant. We're looking for information about a certain piece of jewelry we believe was made by you." Thomas omitted my name for my protection.

"Please, follow me to my office," said the man, suspiciously.

We entered the glass-enclosed office, and he introduced us to his brother, Mr. Shreeve. He was the opposite of Mr. Stephens, short, stocky, with rosy cheeks and quite strong. He looked at me in a strange way, and his scrutinizing gaze made me uncomfortable. I took the liberty and squeezed Thomas's arm, who understood my gesture and placed his hand over mine as a way of protection.

"You mentioned you were interested in a particular piece of jewelry we made," said Mr. Stephens.

I opened my small purse and took out the cufflink, handing it to Thomas.

"Yes, this piece. I was informed that you were the makers. I'm interested in acquiring a pair similar to this model," said Thomas, showing the cufflink to Mr. Stephens.

Of course, Thomas was bluffing; we could never reveal that, in reality, we wanted to find out who owned that object.

When Thomas showed them the jewelry, the brothers exchanged a glance so blatant it was obvious they knew who owned that cufflink.

"Unfortunately, this is an exclusive model made for a very special client, and we are not authorized to make anything similar. If you are interested, I can show you our showcase with other models, which I believe you will find to your liking," said the brother of Mr. Stephens, curtly.

"If it's such an exclusive model, we could ask for personal authorization from your client. Mr. Fawcett would be delighted to do that. Do you agree, Mr. Fawcett?" I said sarcastically.

"Of course! Would you mind providing us with his address?"

"I told you he was a very special client, and I wouldn't want his designs copied, let alone being disturbed. Have a good day!" Mr. Shreeve said sharply.

Mr. Stephens escorted us to the exit, while his brother, showing disdain, headed to the back of the shop with one of his employees.

As we left the store, we walked down the bustling street, looking for a cab. It was then that we saw a Gig racing towards us as fast as it could. It had just turned out of the side street by the shop we'd visited. The coachman drove the horse towards me; I was stunned, unsure where to run, but Thomas quickly pulled me to his side, losing balance and nearly falling to the ground. The carriage passed so close that I felt the horse's mane brush my face, narrowly escaping being run over. Unsatisfied at not achieving his aim, the coachman brandished his whip towards me, cracking it in the air. I felt a searing pain when its tip slashed my arm, leaving a cut.

The carriage then sped down the street until it vanished from sight.

"Rowena, are you hurt?" Thomas asked, concerned.

"My arm still stings from the whip, but the cut is healing. He tried to kill us, Thomas!"

"I saw! He came bursting out from that street next to the shop and charged straight at us, it was all premeditated. Why would he do such a thing?"

"It's all related to the cufflink case. He was an employee of the shop. I noticed when Mr. Shreeve was talking to him at the back of the store. He must have ordered him to attack us," I said, apprehensive. "Look! They're at the door watching us. Please Thomas, let's get out of here as fast as we can."

Thomas hailed a passing cab, helped me in, and we quickly left the scene.

"They were waiting for us. That customer warned them we might show up, so they were on alert. I don't know what this crook told them about us, but it must've been a convincing lie to take the risk of staging a carriage accident to harm or kill us," I said, nervously settled in the carriage.

"With a good bribe, anyone can be bought, Rowena. It's obvious that this special customer handed over a pretty penny to them."

"Now the killer will have a complete description of us. They're going to look for him and notify that we were here," I said worriedly. "We've lost the element of surprise. Ideally, we could've followed these lackeys to the said client. But how could we do that?"

"They only have my name, not yours. I have an idea, Rowena. I'll take you home, and then I'll find Bob Little, to have him and his crew tail these two lunatics. Bob will follow them wherever they go in the next few days."

"Do you think they can do it? They're just kids."

"Of course! They're sharp, and Bob knows how to place his gang at strategic points around the city. This makes it easier to communicate with each other. As they always say, they see everything and know everything. I trust Bob; he's a good kid. Besides, he'll be well compensated, and he knows it.

Thirteen

Thomas dropped me off at home. I found Emily beaming, dressed in her new gowns, fresh from the dressmaker's. They were indeed sharply cut with refined finishes, designed for the upcoming ball season. Emily showed them all to me. I praised them, of course.

"I wasn't about to rain on Emily's parade"

I excused myself and went up to my room. No, I wasn't jealous of Emily and her dresses. They were truly beautiful. I just wasn't much concerned with fashion. I found it dull to spend hours trying on clothes or applying makeup in front of a mirror. In fact, I preferred a good dress that was easy and practical to wear. That's why mine were designed specifically so I could put them on by myself. I rarely needed a maid to help me get ready.

I also wasn't a fan of corsets. Luckily, I had a lean figure. I could almost always do without corsets. They were exceedingly suffocating and weakened our physical structure by squeezing all of our organs. There were many women who fainted from the lack of air they provided. They demanded too much sacrifice for beauty. It was a high price that I was not willing to pay.

I wanted to be free. To have adventures. To become a doctor. Marriage was the last thing on my mind at the moment. Unlike my sister, who was only concerned with social life, parties, and a future husband.

The day after Thomas and I were attacked by the mad driver, Max came to tell me that a boy named Bob was at our gate with a message, insisting on speaking only with me. Max was annoyed by the little guy's audacity of not wanting to leave until I saw him. I calmed Max down, explaining that he was a messenger boy used by Mr. Fawcett, and he likely wanted to deliver a message to me personally.

"Thomas, Thomas, what surprise are you cooking up."

"Max, I'll fetch the message myself. Don't worry," I said firmly.

I went down, opened the gate, and indeed Bob Little was waiting for me. I was apprehensive, Thomas had never sent me messages through this boy. How did he know where I lived?

"Forgive me, Miss Stein, for my boldness in seeking you out. I can't find Thomas, and he made it very clear that as soon as I had any information about the jeweler brothers, I should deliver it to him. If I couldn't find him, I was to immediately seek you out, as he was in a hurry," Bob said, handing me a paper with an address written on it.

"Whose address is this?"

"We've been following the two brothers since yesterday. This was the first address they went to, right after the incident with you. It's in the central district here in London. The other places they went to are mostly their suppliers, from what we gathered."

"Is it a house?"

"No, it's a theater."

"Theater?" I asked, somewhat incredulously.

"Yes, the Adelphi Theater."

"How do you know this is the right address that Thomas is looking for?"

"Because the other addresses were for suppliers, as I mentioned. Here, they weren't buying tickets. They entered through the back. Sought out a woman, quite beautiful by the way. And they returned today to speak with her again."

"Have you found out who this woman is?"

"Miss Darville. The actress Janet Darville."

"An actress! How odd."

"Thank you, Bob, I'll speak with Thomas, and he'll reward you as best as he can."

"Thank you, ma'am," said Bob, tipping his cap slightly as a goodbye.

I was surprised; we were looking for the so-called special client of the jewelers, and they led us to an actress. I didn't understand why the brothers didn't go directly to their client but instead sought an intermediary. Could she be a lover? An accomplice? Or maybe she had no connection at all with the potential killer.

I needed to find out. I would wait for Thomas until dusk, and if he didn't show up, I would go to the theater myself and try to uncover the relationship between this actress and our suspect.

Fourteen

Night had fallen and Thomas was nowhere to be seen. I had put on a lovely dress for the evening. Lucy helped me fashion my hair into a small bun, which I then secured with long silver pins adorned with exquisite jewels. I usually wore them to keep my hat in place. They were my secret weapons, having extricated me from tricky situations before. I descended the stairs, only to be confronted by my father who had just arrived home.

"Great. This is all I needed."

"Good evening, Rowena. Are you planning to go out by any chance? I believe it's rather late for a young lady to be out, especially on her own. I demand an explanation."

"I'm sorry for lying to you, Dad."

"Good evening, Dad. Mr. Thomas Fawcett invited me to the theater. He mentioned that he had asked for your permission. Didn't he?"

"No. Not that I recall. Which theater, and what play was he planning to see?"

"It's an adaptation of a text by Mr. Dickens. At the Adelphi Theatre."

"Dickens, Charles Dickens. I suppose it must be a good play. If I weren't so tired, I'd accompany you." My father altered his tone, then continued. "Do not leave without Mr. Fawcett first having a word with me. Understood?"

"Yes, Dad. As soon as he arrives, I will bring him to you. With your permission, I will get some fresh air in the garden while I wait for Mr. Fawcett."

I went out to the garden and sat on my favorite bench, where I typically got lost in my thoughts.

I was in a bind. I needed to leave. Thomas wouldn't show up, not that night. We hadn't arranged anything. No Thomas. No way out. I got up and very slowly opened the iron gate that led to the street.

"Don't you dare squeak on me now."

I walked briskly to the taxi stand near my residence. I got into the first cab I found.

"Driver, Adelphi Theatre on the Strand. Please."

I leaned back in the seat as the horse began to trot. I breathed a sigh of relief.

"Dad's going to kill me; but that's a story for another day."

We arrived at 411 Strand. The carriage stopped in front of the theatre. The street was bustling, with carriages and people creating a frenetic scene. The driver was polite and helped me alight.

"These long dresses make it so hard to move. We need to create a fashion that's more practical."

"Thank you, sir," I said, paying the coachman.

I had no plan whatsoever. I wasn't even sure if the actress would be at the theatre that night.

The theatre was a three-story building, with pillars flanking the windows of the upper two floors. The entrance consisted of a wide arch. Access to the theatre was on the left, and on the right, between polished granite columns, were the doors leading to its luxurious restaurant.

I had no idea the theatre was so large. Finding Miss Darville would be no easy task.

I headed to the box office. I bought a ticket for the play. Next to me, on the wall, an item on the show's poster caught my attention. Miss

Darville's name was featured prominently. Great, she was in the play, so she was at the theatre.

I pointed at the poster and spoke to the ticket booth attendant.

"I'm a huge fan of the actress Janet Darville, and I'd like to congratulate her on her flawless performance."

"Good heavens, I'm headed straight for hell. I don't even know this actress."

"Miss, she's currently in her dressing room, getting ready for the show. She seldom meets anyone before a performance. You might have better luck catching her right after the show ends."

"Please, where can I find the dressing rooms?"

"At the end of the private box gallery, on the side where the women's dressing rooms are. But as I told you, after the performance would be better."

I thanked the young man and headed in the direction he indicated. I needed to speak with the actress before the play started. I couldn't stay until the end of the show. It would be too late for me to get home alone, and likely my father would be extremely upset, waiting for a good explanation.

The gallery of private boxes was sumptuous. The softness of the carpet muffled the noisy steps of gentlemen and ladies, all dressed to the nines, who walked through the hallway in search of their respective private boxes.

As I passed a box with its door open, I noticed it was empty. Curiosity killed the cat – wanting to see the grandeur of the Adelphi stage, which I was unfamiliar with, got the better of me. I entered the box and walked up to its balcony; the splendor of the theater took my breath away. The chandelier lights reflected off the women's necklaces and bracelets, creating a dazzling kaleidoscope of colors, and for a few moments, I was mesmerized by the sight before me.

At that moment, a hand grabbed my arm. I startled, and just as I was about to scream...

"Easy, Rowena. It's me, Thomas. Did you think I was the killer?" he asked mockingly.

"Darn it, if there were ever a time, I wished I wasn't a lady. This would be it."

"You scared me. What are you doing here?"

"The same thing as you. To talk to Miss Darville. Bob managed to find me and passed me the address. I figured your curiosity would bring you here."

Thomas saw me enter the theater and followed me. He was also looking for the actress. Thomas's family owned a private box at the Adelphi, so he was well-acquainted with the theater's entire structure. We quickly found the dressing room of the actress Janet Darville.

The door of the dressing room was slightly ajar. Thomas gently knocked on the door. We waited. No answer. Thomas pushed the door a bit further. We entered.

Miss Darville was lying on a moss-green sofa with beautiful floral prints. A cut from one end of her throat to the other fed a thick stream of blood, which ran down her limp arm, dangling towards the floor. A pool of blood was forming on the carpet.

"There would be no show that night."

Thomas and I were stunned. He walked over to the actress's body to examine her, to see if she was still breathing. I, still in shock, remained standing at the entrance of the dressing room, with my back to the half-open door.

A noise behind the door alerted me, but it was too late. Someone pulled my arm backward, holding me tightly. And then, a blood-stained knife was pressed against my face. It was surely the killer of Miss Darville.

He was hiding behind the door. He had just murdered the actress and hid when we arrived. He wore a small mask to conceal his identity. He probably grabbed it from the dressing room when he heard our voices approaching.

I stammered

"Thomas, please..."

Thomas turned in my direction, but the criminal, backing away with me, had already moved out of the dressing room. My friend tried to react, but the instinct of the person holding me drove him to stab the knife into my face. A trickle of blood ran down my cheek. I felt pain and moaned.

Thomas stopped.

The murderer was walking backwards, taking me as a hostage. With one hand, he firmly held my arm twisted behind my back, causing me immense pain, and with the other, he kept the knife near my face.

We moved slowly backwards, step by step, toward the rear of the theater. There was a private stage door there, a place where artists entered the Adelphi.

Thomas followed us, keeping some distance, perhaps afraid that something worse might happen to me.

Upon reaching the door, still with the knife near my face, the criminal released my arm to open the door. In this moment of distraction, I pulled out one of the pins holding my hair up and with the same movement, I drove it with all my strength, several times into his hand, the one that held the knife.

"Damn you!" he screamed horribly. The pain made him drop the knife, while he pushed me, causing me to fall to the ground.

In seconds, he opened the door and fled. Thomas ran to me, helped me up, and we opened the door to Maiden Lane. Too late, the murderer had entered a carriage that was waiting for him, with an accomplice inside. They sped away.

The blood on my face had coagulated and the wound from the knife had healed. Thomas took out his handkerchief and cleaned my face. Then he hugged me. My whole body was shaking. Not with desire. But with fear. An immense fear of what was to come.

Fifteen

When Thomas felt me shiver, he pressed his body closer to mine. He lifted my chin with the tips of his fingers and planted a chaste kiss on my cheek, where the knife had pricked me.

"Calm down, Rowena. You're safe," he said.

"I know. But I can't stop shaking."

"We better head back to Miss Darville's dressing room; maybe we'll find a clue to why she was murdered," Thomas said, holding my hand.

"Or her connection to the jewelers," I said, more calmly.

Thomas kissed my face without my permission. I wasn't offended. It was his way of showing I was protected. Furthermore, I felt comforted in his arms. The world could crumble around us, and I wouldn't care. It was as if it was just him and me against the world.

As we walked towards the dressing room, a murmur of voices reached us. They belonged to people gathered near the crime scene, all curious to see the victim. We cautiously approached the door.

"Miss Stein and Mr. Fawcett. What are you doing here?" Inspector Tennyson asked from inside the dressing room.

"We came to watch the play, then heard about the crime," Thomas replied.

"How did you find out about the murder so quickly?" I asked the inspector.

"I was in the theater. I was also going to watch the play. They informed me that the murderer took a girl as a hostage to facilitate his escape. Do you know anything about it?"

"No. We were on our way to speak with Miss Darville when someone informed us about the crime," I lied without remorse.

The Inspector didn't need to know that I was the girl used as a hostage. Nor that we saw the murderer. And least of all that the real reason we were at the theater was because we were investigating. If he suspected anything, he would likely interrogate us until dawn. And my father would be informed of all these events, since I was directly involved with the criminal. It wouldn't be good for me.

The Inspector let us go. I asked Thomas to take me home. I needed him to escort me and to come up with a good excuse for Dr. Robert, since I left without his permission.

"Good evening, Mr. Fawcett," Max said, with a stern expression, as he opened the door for us.

"Max, where is father?"

"The doctor just arrived, he's in the library waiting for you. He's not in the best of moods."

"He just got here. Where was he?"

Upon arriving at the library, my father stood up angrily. Without even greeting Thomas, as if no one was with me, he spoke harshly:

"Well, well, Miss Rowena Duncan Stein. What did we agree on? I said you would only go out when Mr. Thomas came to talk to me. But no, what did you do? You sneaked out at night, without my permission."

"I'm sorry, Dr. Robert, it's my fault. I had a mishap with my carriage and arrived at your house too close to the theater's start time. Since Miss Stein was waiting in the garden, I persuaded her to come with me, so we wouldn't be even later. I promised that I would take full responsibility with you later."

"Thomas, you know this is not the way a gentleman behaves. Even if you were late for the play, you should have spoken to me," my father said, still angry. "Besides, why did you come back early? Didn't stay until the end of the play?"

"There was an incident at the theater," I said cautiously.

"Incident. What kind?"

"A murder."

"Murder. What do you mean?"

"The actress Janet Darville, was murdered."

"Miss Darville, sister to Jo Darville?" my father asked, with indignation, sinking back into the sofa seat.

Thomas and I exchanged glances; what amateur detectives we were. We hadn't even made the connection between the actresses' surnames. Surely there was some link they had with the young women's deaths.

"Did you know both of them?" I asked, fearing the answer.

"Yes. Mrs. Jo Darville was the partner of a close friend of mine, also a doctor. He has passed away. Poor thing, she recently lost her daughter. And now her sister."

Dr. Robert's attention shifted to the two sisters, making him forget the reprimand he was giving. Thomas mentioned that Inspector Tennyson was at the theater and had taken charge of the investigation. My father, of course, wanted more details. I excused myself from the two of them and went up to my room to rest, as I was very tired, leaving the finer points to Thomas.

The next morning, I was in the office with my father, who was telling me about a lecture he had given a few days ago, when Max informed us that Inspector Tennyson was waiting in the living room.

"Bring him here, Max."

I got up and was heading to the door when the Inspector came in and greeted us.

"Miss Stein, a pleasure to see you. I would like to ask you some questions. That is, if the doctor doesn't mind?"

I looked at my father, who nodded for me to stay. I sat down on a sofa opposite his desk.

"Please, Inspector, have a seat," I said.

"Some witnesses described the woman who the murderer took hostage yesterday. And the description matches you, including the color of your dress."

Dr. Robert's eyebrows nearly met in a serious look he directed at me.

"Explain yourself, Rowena Stein."

"Well, now, Rowena, get out of this pickle."

"As I told you yesterday, Inspector, Mr. Fawcett and I were indeed near Janet Darville's dressing room because we wanted to congratulate her. As for the color of my dress and my appearance, I consider them to be common. There were several young ladies looking similar and wearing dresses of the same color as mine. Someone must have seen me near the scene and jumped to wild conclusions. I assure you we saw nothing."

"I was informed that the young lady was taken hostage and her companion tried to protect her. Since the descriptions matched you and your friend, I was intrigued. That's the reason for my visit."

"For the last time, I will tell you exactly what happened. We were approaching the actress's dressing room when people started arriving, talking about someone's death. As we got closer, we learned that the victim was Miss Janet Darville. We entered the dressing room to confirm the rumors and found you. That's the truth."

"But miss, the witnesses..."

"Please, Inspector, do you prefer to trust strangers who, caught up in the moment, make up stories, over me? Besides, if I had been the victim of that madman, I would provide all the descriptions possible, so you could catch him as quickly as possible."

"Enough, Inspector Tennyson! You are embarrassing my daughter. She has clarified everything for you. Yet, you persist in accusing her of something that, had it happened, Rowena would have been the victim, not to blame. Have a good day, Inspector."

My father rang the bell, and Max appeared to escort the Inspector out. He left, annoyed with me. Mr. Tennyson was known for overstepping his bounds, usually intimidating those he interrogated. I was no criminal. I had merely witnessed a crime. One that I didn't want and couldn't report.

Things were taking a turn I did not like. They began to spiral out of control. The murderer was, without a doubt, after me, seeking my blood. And that scared me. The Inspector, with his arrogance, couldn't see the forest for the trees, failing to connect the dots. I couldn't help him; I couldn't reveal my secret to him.

"You really didn't get involved in this mess, did you, Rowena?"

"Of course not, Dad. We just went to meet the actress and stumbled upon this unpleasant event."

Sixteen

Aunt Annie arrived that afternoon, all aglow, to have tea with us. Her eyes sparkled with a special shine, radiating happiness. Mary Penny arranged a beautiful and delicious tea table for us. Emily, burning with curiosity to know why auntie was so cheerful, was the first to sit at the table. I took my usual seat, and Aunt Annie faced us both. Auntie has always been joyful, it was rare to see her sad, but today, she seemed like she was at peace with the world.

"Girls, do you remember that knight who took me out to dance at the Holyhead ball?"

"Of course, the one you danced with three times in a row," Emily chimed in.

"He's an English Lord, staying for some time in Paris. He has proposed to me."

"Did you accept?" I asked, nibbling on a biscuit.

"He's returning to Paris this week. I've agreed to accompany him, so we can get to know each other a bit more."

"Do you think it's wise to go to another country with someone you barely know?"

"Lord William Chapman is a gentleman, Rowena. He will respect me while I am a guest in his house. Moreover, we will be getting married in no time."

"I'll have a stunning dress made for your wedding."

"It's not necessary, Emily. I'll be getting married in Paris. It's probable my brother won't be able to go, and he wouldn't let you travel alone."

"Oh! Paris. Dad has to go; it will be a wonderful trip. Don't you think, Rowena?"

"He's very busy, Emily. It will depend a lot on his commitments at the time. Anyway, aunt, I hope you're very happy."

"And I will miss our afternoon tea chats," said Emily sincerely.

Max went to answer the door. It was dad, coming in just as we were having tea, he joined us.

"We were just talking about you, Robert," said auntie.

"Auntie Annie is getting married. Did you know?" asked Emily.

"Yes, she had told me."

"And you didn't tell us," said Emily.

"Because I still hoped she would give up this crazy adventure. Moving in with a stranger, in another country, and then to get married. Who does that?"

"Brother, you're being unfair. I'm not moving in with Lord Chapman. He's welcoming me as a guest in his house. He promised to treat me with all respect. His commitments in Paris are not few, making it difficult for him to come to London all the time. Nor can I go to Paris whenever, as you know, the costs are high. That's why we agreed I would spend some time in France, to get to know each other better before getting married."

"And what did our father think of all this?" Dr. Robert inquired.

"At first, he was hesitant, but I am twenty-eight years old. By our standards, I'm considered a spinster. So, dad eventually agreed. Widowhood has made him increasingly bitter. Furthermore, in the few days I spent with Lord Chapman, he proved to be a kind and respectful man."

"We will go to the wedding. Won't we, dad?" Emily asked, breaking the tension in the air.

"When a date is set, we'll think about it, my dear. I don't know what commitments I'll have at that time."

My father wished his sister happiness. He excused himself, as he had to leave again to attend to a patient who required his care. He went to his office, grabbed his medical bag, and left. I called Mary Penny to bring us more hot tea, and we continued talking about the wonders of Paris.

Auntie had left a while ago, and Emily went up to her room, determined to finish painting one of her canvases. I headed to the library and was flipping through the newspaper when Max informed me that Inspector Tennyson wanted to have a word with me.

"Did you tell him dad wasn't here?" I asked anxiously.

"Yes, but he insisted on speaking with you. If you like, I can ask him to come back when Dr. Robert is home."

"No need, Max. Bring him here. Let's see what's so urgent it can't wait for dad. Stay close in case I need you."

Inspector Tennyson entered the library, and I heard Max's discreet cough from a nearby corridor, signaling he was on standby if I needed his assistance.

"Good afternoon, Miss Stein. Sorry for the disturbance."

"How can I help you? Dad is not in," I said, folding the newspaper I was reading and placing it on the side table.

"It's about that actress's case."

"Inspector, that matter was cleared up the last time you were here," I said apprehensively.

"Yes. Yes. Of course. But did you know she was pregnant?"

"Pregnant? But why would I know that? I didn't even know Miss Darville."

"But your father knew her. She might have mentioned something to him. Perhaps the name of her lover."

Inspector thought everyone had a dirty mind, like his. My father would never delve into such intimate matters with the actress, even if they were close. Or if he had such a confession from a patient, he wouldn't go around spreading it. Certainly not to me. The inspector was beginning to show disrespect. This was not a conversation for a lady.

"Sorry, inspector, but you are mistaken. Dr. Robert is Mrs. Jo Darville's doctor, the sister. Not the murdered actress."

"I know, but sisters confide in each other. He might have overheard something."

"Then you would have to ask him, or better yet directly Mrs. Jo Darville." I was losing patience with the inspector's lack of manners. "Are you calling me and my father gossipmongers?"

"Forgive me, miss. Of course not. It's just that I see this death from a different angle. I don't believe the motive for this crime is the same as for those young ladies who were killed."

"Why do you think so?"

"Actress Janet Darville was much older than those three girls, who I believe were virgins. She was pregnant and did not have any birthmarks on her body."

"Who do you attribute this crime to?"

"To the lover. Of course."

"Then arrest her boyfriend!" I said aggressively, out of patience with the inspector.

"It's not that simple, miss. No one wants to give me that information."

"Or maybe they really don't know who he might be. Don't you agree, inspector?"

I rang the bell, and Max promptly appeared before me. I asked him to show Inspector Tennyson out. Mr. Tennyson left reluctantly, but he finally left.

Indeed, the way he was viewing the crime seemed correct. The actress's death wasn't for the same reason as the others. Could it be a different killer?

I was still in the library when my father returned. I heard him in the vestibule scolding Max, who shortly after appeared, informing me that

Dr. Robert was waiting for me in his office. Max was pale; the earful he received must have been quite severe. I hoped it had nothing to do with me.

"Good evening, Father. You wanted to see me?" I entered and closed the door behind me.

"I just found out from Max that Inspector Tennyson was here after I left. Did he have the audacity to speak to you without me being present?"

"Yes. He insisted on speaking with me."

"But what on earth did he need to discuss with you so urgently?"

"It was about the death of actress Janet Darville."

"Damn. He's still harping on about that subject."

"The autopsy found that she was pregnant. And he wanted to know if you knew the name of her lover."

"The inspector has lost his marbles. That's a topic he never should have broached with you, especially not in private. I've spoken to Max and told him that he's only allowed to enter this house when I'm present. It was completely disrespectful of him to approach you like that."

"He thought that since you were the doctor of her sister, you might have heard something about Miss Janet Darville's boyfriend."

"Jo Darville, the nutcase? I doubt it. Speaking of which, I was just tending to her and during one of her rare moments of clarity, she mentioned that a young couple of journalists from The Express had interviewed her a few days ago. She couldn't remember their names, but she described you and Thomas perfectly. And Thomas is from The Express. What were you doing there?"

"Mr. Fawcett was working on a piece about former theatre actresses. She was going to be one of his next interviews, and it was by chance that he saw you entering Mrs. Jo Darville's house. So, he mentioned it to me. We didn't know you were her doctor. I'm sorry, Father, I thought she was your girlfriend. So, I asked Mr. Fawcett to take me as his assistant."

"Rowena, you're going to hell with your lies."

My father burst out laughing, and said:

"The girlfriend of that madwoman. Only in your wildest dreams, Rowena." He stopped laughing and became serious. "Wait! Was it she who told you about the adoption?"

"Yes. She had no idea I was your daughter, and in one of her delusions, she mentioned that her lover and Dr. Robert, who were friends, had brought a baby from Germany, which you ended up adopting. So, I came home looking for clues about who this child could be. I found out it was me."

"My God! What a terrible way to find out you were adopted! I'm sorry, my dear, I never wanted you to find out. Certainly not like this."

Max knocked on the door, and entered carrying a tray with a note that demanded an immediate response. My father quickly wrote a reply and handed it to the butler.

"I need to leave, Rowena, but our conversation isn't over."

My father stood up and we walked to his study. While he was packing his bag, I asked:

"Has something serious happened?"

"It's Mr. George Holyhead. Just over a year ago, he was in Calcutta, and contracted a severe form of malaria. He nearly saw death's door. He was left with serious aftereffects and developed a form of migraine that's the most aggressive, rendering him almost delirious at times. During these episodes, he becomes very aggressive due to the pain he feels in his head and eyes."

"But he is a doctor, and so is Dr. Holyhead, his father. Why are you the one who must see him?"

"Dr. Henry Holyhead is out of London. The note was from his wife, asking for my help. As for George, poor fellow, during these crises, he locks himself in his room in the dark, completely losing touch with reality. If you could see him, with his bloodshot eyes, you'd think he was a monster. But the treatment I'm going to give him is just palliative, it merely eases the crisis."

"Willow bark powder?"

"It's no longer effective. It only reduces the fever. For the migraine, he's unfortunately already on laudanum, with a higher concentration of opium."

"Opium! My goodness!"

"I must go." My father took his bag and left.

Seventeen

The morning was off, accompanied by a heavy feel in the air that painted the sky a dull gray. I walked through the gardens of Gordon Square, right across from my house, enjoying the sight of nannies in their spotless uniforms taking their charges for a stroll in the park, all neat and bundled up. I admired the discreet bravery of young lovers exchanging love letters. I basked in the beauty and peace of the place while waiting for Thomas, pondering over recent events.

I jumped when someone tapped my shoulder.

"Lost in thought, Rowena?"

"Just trying to calm my mind."

"I was worried when I received your message," Thomas said. "Why arrange to meet here and not in your house?"

"Emily is rather restless today, and I needed some privacy."

"What happened?"

"My father found out yesterday we visited Mrs. Jo Darville. I had to confirm we went as journalists. I made up the excuse that I thought they were involved romantically, so I visited her."

"Did you talk to him about the adopted baby?"

"Of course not. It would have put him in an awkward position. Besides, I've discovered nothing about the adopted child yet."

"Sorry Thomas, but that's a secret you can't know."

We walked slowly while talking. Thomas, with his arms behind his back and head down, paid close attention to our conversation.

"Inspector Tennyson looked for me yesterday," I said.

"Another murder?"

"No. The autopsy of actress Janet Darville revealed she was pregnant."

"I know. He also questioned me if I knew anything about it. Sorry, he was rather blunt in discussing this with you."

As we were still walking, a figure caught my eye. Someone was leaving our house. It was Mary Penny, carrying a basket covered with a cloth that seemed heavy. She looked back as she left to see if anyone was following her. She quickly walked toward the same taxi stand I had used a few times.

"Thomas, did you come in your carriage?"

"Yes. Why?"

"Would you join me in a pursuit? But it must be now."

Thomas's carriage was parked very close to my house. We got in just in time to see Mary Penny departing in a taxi. I quickly explained to Thomas why we were following my governess, and he instructed his driver to keep a certain distance from the other carriage.

Penny's taxi took a northbound turn toward Pentoville, taking Liverpool Road, and heading toward the suburbs of Islington. I began to wonder where this chase would end up, and what was the importance of this person in Penny's life, for her to risk such a long race, possibly losing her job. Just after a lush tree, with branches seeming to embrace the road, Penny's carriage turned right onto a small street, stopping in front of a row of semi-detached houses with visible red bricks. She got out and entered the door where a young woman, holding a baby, waited for her. Penny wouldn't take long, as the driver waited for her. We also waited, a bit away, to remain undiscovered. Some time later, the governess appeared without the basket, entered the taxi, and left.

Thomas and I got out of the carriage and walked up to the house she had entered. I knocked softly on the door, and the same young woman answered.

"Good morning, I'm Miss Ruth Madras," I made up a name. "I'm with the parish ministry of St. Mary Magdalene, under Father Hughes. May we come in?"

"Of course, please come in, Miss."

The house was modest; the living room was clean. My gaze discreetly swept over the young woman, the baby in her arms, everything around me, and finally landed on a small table where the basket that Penny had brought was resting. Peeking inside it revealed; eggs, hams, and a few other food items.

"Our parish is registering some needy families in the area to provide assistance. I believe you might not be in need," I implied, nodding towards the basket on the table.

Awkwardly, she covered the basket with the cloth that Mary Penny had brought.

"No, please. My mother brought this basket today. But she can't always help us. Of course, any help is always welcome. Especially with the newborn baby."

"Your mother doesn't live with you?"

"No! She visits us occasionally. And with the birth of the baby, I haven't been able to work, and the child's father has abandoned us."

Why hadn't Penny told me her daughter was in need, instead of stealing food from our pantry? I fished for a pencil and a piece of paper in my bag, and to add more credibility to the fake registration, I asked the young woman for some details, confirmed her name and her parentage. Indeed, she was Mary Penny's daughter, and I promised that the church would help her, although, of course, it was I who would take it upon myself to ensure that we did. First, I would have a very serious conversation with Mary Penny.

On our way back to Gordon Square, via Liverpool Road, we encountered a minor accident that had just occurred, involving a farmer's cart. The axle of its rear wheels had broken, and a green sea of vegetables and greens had spilled onto the road, rendering it impassable. Children and even adults were filling their arms, delighted at the prospect of a much more nutritious soup that evening. To the cart owner's despair, who cursed and swore as his goods were pilfered before his eyes.

Thomas asked our driver to turn right onto Cloudesley Square, to escape the chaos we had found ourselves in. Entering the street, we were greeted by a tranquil and pleasant square, a stark contrast to the confusion we had just left. In its center, a lush hexagonal garden surrounded Holy Trinity Church. We circled the church to exit through the square's opposite entrance. A carriage coming in the opposite direction to ours stopped well before crossing paths with us. The driver pulled out the steps, and a lady alighted with confidence and an upright posture. She walked with assured steps towards a house. She unlocked the door with her key and disappeared inside.

"That's Mrs. Gertie Holyhead. I thought she was bedridden," I commented, surprised. "Thomas, could you ask your coachman to stop, please?"

Thomas knocked twice on the roof, and we stopped a little past the Holyhead's carriage, which had moved onto a side street. It looked like Mrs. Holyhead was going to be awhile.

"Did you see that, Thomas?" I asked as I got out of the carriage.

"Yes, she was walking perfectly without the support of her customary cane. Very strange," Thomas was baffled. "She was an excellent horsewoman, but about two years ago, she had an accident when she fell from her horse, seriously injuring her pelvis. She can't walk without her cane because of the pain. That's why she's been so reclusive."

"She didn't seem so reclusive to me. Could she be faking it for her husband? Perhaps this is a rendezvous spot for some illicit affair with a lover?" I mused.

"I'd like to know as well. Our newspaper did a piece on it at the time. The husband even sued the club. But it led nowhere. Do you think she has a lover?"

"She's still young and beautiful. But why fake it for everyone? And whose house is that? She entered with her own key."

"I'll ask Bob Little and the boys to comb through this place, just out of curiosity. Mrs. Holyhead's behavior is quite suspicious."

"Do you think it's right to pry into her life?"

"Rowena, have you forgotten I'm a journalist? It's my job to snoop around."

As we climbed back into the carriage to leave, I took one last look at the house and noticed a slight movement in the curtains of one of the rooms.

"Thomas, the bedroom curtain just moved. Someone was watching us."

Thomas glanced toward the house, but all was quiet. If someone had been lurking, they had vanished.

Thomas dropped me off at my house and went off in search of Bob.

"Max, has Penny arrived yet?"

"Yes, miss."

"I'm in my room waiting for her."

I pulled up a chair and sat down at my desk, needing to write some letters. I still hadn't figured out why Mrs. Holyhead had played the part of a paralytic. Penny knocked and entered.

"You wanted to see me, Miss Stein? Max told me you wished to speak with me."

"Mrs. Butler told me that some food has been disappearing from our pantry. Did she tell you?"

"Yes, but I believe it's more likely due to her own wastefulness when preparing meals. She fails to notice it. That's why I didn't take her complaints seriously."

"Mrs. Butler has been with us for many years. One of her qualities is not wasting food; on the contrary, she's quite frugal. And you know that."

"What do you mean?"

"I want the truth, Mary Penny," I demanded authoritatively.

"I don't understand, miss," she said, blushing.

"I know you've been leaving with food in a basket."

"Are you accusing me of being a thief?"

"Not yet. I just want to know what's happening."

"I know everything, Penny. Please, open up to me."

Penny lowered her head, and her hands couldn't stay still as she tried to adjust her uniform, showing her nervousness.

"I have a daughter, she recently had a baby, and her husband, a good-for-nothing, abandoned her shortly after the birth. As a result, she's struggling because she can't work. Who would hire her with a newborn baby? Luckily, the house is mine, so she doesn't have to pay rent. I help as much as I can, but sometimes money is tight. That's why I took some food for her and the child. I intended to replace it as soon as I could, but Mrs. Butler noticed it was missing."

"It was easier to blame her," I said, annoyed.

"No, please forgive me, miss, I didn't mean to. I've never taken anything from this house. It was just the desperation of seeing my daughter in need."

"Why didn't you ask me, or even my father?"

"I don't know. I was afraid. As I said, I was planning to replace it. Are you going to dismiss me?"

"I should, because what you did was theft. And you know that for much less a boss would fire their servant. But doing so would only worsen your situation, and that of your daughter and grandchild. I see only one way for you to stay with us."

"What is it, Miss Stein?"

"You're no longer allowed to leave without my permission, except on your day off, as previously agreed. I want you to apologize to Mrs. Butler immediately. There's no need to tell her you were the one taking the food. And I will not tolerate any more quarrels between you and Mrs. Butler."

"Thank you for your understanding, miss."

"As for your daughter, I won't leave her in the lurch. Max, and only Max, will prepare a generous basket weekly, with fruits, vegetables, eggs, and cake, for you to take to her on your day off on Sunday. Now, be warned. Any more slip-ups, and I'll immediately inform my father. And I assure you, Dr. Robert won't be as forgiving."

Mary Penny, still embarrassed, thanked me again, informing that she was going to the kitchen to apologize to the cook. How she was going to do that without admitting her guilt, I didn't know. At least I was sure, for a while there wouldn't be any gossip or arguments between the two.

Eighteen

I woke up to the distant sounds of children laughing and playing. I walked over to my window and caught sight of a brightly overcast sky. It seemed like we were in for a rather pleasant day. The voices and laughter that reached my ears belonged to the little ones and their nannies, joyously running across the fresh grass of Gordon Square. They were playing hide and seek behind the lush trees, driving their guardians mad trying to find them.

A wave of nostalgia for my childhood overcame me, as I remembered, how Emily and I used to run through these same lawns, hiding from each other, and even from dad, making him search for where we were hidden. My goodness, how happy we were with so little.

Lily knocked on my door and came in, surprised to see me up so early. I've always been quite the sleeper. I asked about Emily. She was still asleep. I asked Lily to bring in the coffee while I got dressed. I was determined to make the most of the day. I hadn't had any nightmares, and woke up cherishing good memories of my childhood with Emily.

I was enjoying the coffee brought by Lily while she did my hair.

"Is Dad seeing a patient in his office?"

"No, miss. He's in the study."

The study's door was slightly ajar; I peeked inside, where my father was leafing through some papers on his desk.

"Good morning, Dad. Are you busy?"

"Just routine stuff, come in."

I sat down, and with great tact, asked about the accident, Mrs. Gertie Holyhead's fall from her horse. At first, he wondered why I was interested. Then he recounted everything just as Thomas had told me.

"Do you honestly think she's truly crippled?"

"What brings you to doubt this? Do you know something?"

"Mr. Fawcett has been assisting me with some charity work. We've been delivering food to families in need..."

"Sorry for the lie, Dad."

"I wasn't aware of that, but please continue."

"Yesterday, as we were passing by Cloudesley Square, we saw Mrs. Gertie alighting from her carriage, in front of a house, walking unaided by her cane, with strong and perfectly assured steps. Even with a certain grace in her stride."

"Are you sure it was her? That's impossible, since the accident she's always used a cane because she experiences a lot of pain while walking. Tries to spend as little time on her feet as possible."

"We found it odd. Could she be putting on an act for Dr. Holyhead? Could she have a lover?"

"This is all news to me. Over the past two years, she's presented herself as a suffering and incapacitated woman. But now that you mention it, every time I've seen her, her complexion was always radiant and beautiful. Not the appearance of someone tormented by pain." My father grew pensive. "No, I can't believe she's faking it and Dr. Holyhead isn't aware."

Max appeared at the door

"Excuse me, Dr. Robert. Inspector Tennyson is waiting for you in the living room."

"What a nuisance! That man never leaves us in peace," my father grumbled.

I stood up to leave.

"Stay, Rowena. I need to reprimand him for his disrespect towards you the other day. And I want you to be present."

After the usual greetings, and my father scolded him for his disrespectful attitude towards me. Mr. Tennyson turned sarcastic.

"Forgive me, Dr. Robert, but my suspicions were not entirely unfounded."

"How so, Inspector?" my father asked, taken aback.

"I've discovered who was actress Janet Darville's lover, and possibly her killer."

"Who?"

"Dr. Robert Duncan. And you must have killed her upon finding out she was pregnant with your child."

"You're out of your mind!" my father exclaimed as he stood up, pounding the table.

"Does the Doctor deny having an affair with Miss Janet Darville?"

"I deny it! I never had an affair with her. We were dating. Miss Janet was single, and I was a widower. There were no obstacles, so we were not lovers but engaged to each other," my father looked at me, his face flushed with anger and shame for being in my presence. "How far along did the autopsy determine the pregnancy to be?"

"Nearly three months."

"But that just proves how delusional you are. We ended things almost six months ago. And after the breakup, we never saw each other again. As you can see, there's no way this child could be mine. The father of this baby is definitely the lover you're so desperately looking for. And he is undoubtedly the murderer of poor Miss Darville."

"Why did you two end the relationship?"

"That's neither here nor there at the moment. Nor is it any of your concern. Knock on another door and search for the child's father, and you'll find your killer. Next time, be more thorough in your investigations. Good day, inspector, we have nothing more to discuss," my father, visibly distressed, sat down, rang the bell, and Max escorted Mr. Tennyson, still dumbfounded, outside.

I had never seen my father so hostile. Without a second thought, he opened the drawer, took out a round blue pill from a tin, which had caught my attention the other day, and then swallowed it dry.

"Are you ill?"

"I'd rather not talk about it now. You've heard too many personal things today. I'd like to be alone for a while.

"Of course, dad.

My father was right. The inspector had brought up intimate details he probably wouldn't have wanted his daughters to know about. He never discussed his flirtation with Miss Janet with us. But it was the pills that worried me, having read about them in a pharmaceutical manual, and knowing their main component was dangerous and deadly. This had scared me.

I headed to the library, anxious to research more on the subject. Emily had woken up, and I found her, arbitrarily flipping through a fashion magazine. She was in a good mood, and we chatted about trivial things.

"Excuse me, Miss Stein. A message for you," Max entered, bringing a sealed note on a tray. "The messenger is waiting for a reply."

I opened the message; it was from Miss Joanna, Thomas's sister, inviting us for afternoon tea at her home. She was particularly interested in having Emily come along. I found the invitation odd, given we were not close. Could this be one of Thomas's jokes? Max sent off our response, and I passed the invitation to Emily, who was eager to read the note's contents.

"An afternoon at Thomas's house. Of course we'll go, Rowena."

Our carriage took the westward path on New Road, rounded the landscaped squares of Park Crescent, and descended the wide avenue of Portland Place, leading us to the Fawcett residence. Its Georgian style, with its beautiful white windows set against an oasis of plants, flowers, and shrubs, welcomed us warmly. Miss Joanna Fawcett, with her beauty and grace, apologized for her parents' absence, making Emily and me feel quite at home. It was as if we had been friends for years.

We talked about life's frivolities, her concerns about being introduced to society next year, the upcoming ball season, and we laughed at two or three suitors who were currently courting her. Emily, of course, felt right at home; this was her favorite topic.

Thomas, who was in his office drafting some piece for the newspaper, came to join us as soon as tea was served. He was accompanied by a young man whose face seemed vaguely familiar.

"Good afternoon, ladies," said Thomas with his usual touch of irony, bowing slightly.

"Rowena and Emily, this is Mr. Edmund Crotch. A family friend. He was with us at the Holyhead ball," Joanna said with her enchanting smile.

It was the young man whom Emily had bluntly refused to dance with when Joanna introduced us at the ball. A thought dawned on me, the real reason behind Joanna's invitation. Mr. Crotch must be interested in Emily, and Thomas's sister had set up this meeting. I extended my hand in greeting and then Emily, who rolled her eyes with subtle disapproval, as he took the tips of her fingers and bowed.

"Emily, Emily, don't embarrass me."

Between one cup of hot tea and the next, and nibbling on some quince-coated biscuits, the conversation went on smoothly. Mr. Crotch was all praises for Emily, laughing at even the slightest folly she said. Emily felt like the center of attention, her ego was through the roof. Joanna laughed at the whole situation.

Thomas excused himself and invited me to his office, wanting to show me some documents. I was curious. His office was spacious, with furniture of exquisite taste, clearly bearing his sister's touch. Shelves full of books covered one wall. Over the fireplace hung a collection of pistols and daggers. In one corner, a human skeleton startled me; it looked like it had been taken from a morgue or perhaps a tomb long ago, which I was in no hurry to learn more about. On his polished mahogany desk were scattered papers, presumably the piece he had been writing for the newspaper. That was Thomas for you.

He leaned against the door, leaving it ajar so I wouldn't feel uncomfortable, and said:

"Bob Little is missing."

"Missing. What do you mean?"

"Remember the suspicious house of Mrs. Gertie?"

"Yes, you were going to have Bob keep an eye on it. "

"One of the boys, who was supposed to take over from Bob yesterday, didn't find him at the agreed spot. He came to see me today, worried."

"Bob probably got caught up in some boys' scuffle and went home hurt."

"They went to Bob's house. He hasn't shown up there. Bob would never leave his post without someone to take his place. I'm worried."

"What do you plan to do?"

"I don't know. I'm thinking about visiting the house tomorrow."

"You're going to break in?"

"If the opportunity arises."

"You're mad, Thomas! Breaking and entering is a crime. You could get arrested, and you don't even know if the boy is in that house. Why not call the police?"

"With what excuse? 'Look officer, the wife of one of London's top surgeons is holding a child captive in a house that I don't even know who lives in.' It doesn't add up, Rowena."

"He's a street kid. He can take care of himself," I tried to ease Thomas's frustration.

"You don't understand. Bob has helped me with many investigations for the newspaper. He and his gang have got me out of many tight spots, you included. If he's in danger, it's my turn to help him. Now, that house seems even more suspicious to me."

I began to understand the fondness Thomas had for young Bob, considering the boy like a younger brother who needed protection. What he didn't understand was that, despite his young age, Bob, having been raised on the streets, was much stronger and smarter than my friend thought. I couldn't let Thomas, in the heat of the moment, do something foolish.

"I'll come with you."

"Over my dead body! If I get caught, I can pretend to be a nosy journalist to defend myself. You're a young lady; if you get caught, your reputation will be tarnished," Thomas held my hand in his. "I don't want that for you."

My face turned red, but I didn't pull my hand away.

"We'll be careful, we won't get caught," I said, looking into Thomas's eyes.

The maid knocked at the door. I composed myself. She informed us that Emily would like to leave.

As we returned to Garden Square, Emily entered the carriage with a displeased expression, despite having bid Thomas a very lively farewell. I mentioned that we had a very pleasant afternoon.

"Well, maybe for you, who was locked away with Thomas in his study."

"Emily, he was just showing me a new article he wrote for the newspaper. And the door wasn't locked. You're slandering me."

"You think I don't realize Joanna invited us just to set me up with that scrawny Edmund Crotch."

"He's a handsome young man, not scrawny at all, and moreover, he's much older than you. His grandfather is a renowned composer; he must have a romantic soul. Why not give him a chance?"

"I won't deny Mr. Crotch is charming and gentlemanly. And the conversation with Joanna was pleasant. But you know where my interests lie."

Emily's obsession with Thomas irked me. She knew he was interested in me. And she knew I was receptive to his attentions. Yet, she continued to believe that with her beauty, she could have Mr. Fawcett at her feet in a heartbeat. But Emily had yet to realize that she was only 14, grown up yet still a girl, hardly of age to date, let alone marry. My sister's immaturity got on my nerves. Dad had spoiled Emily too much. Sooner or later, I would have to bring this issue to his attention. Of course, Dr. Robert would make me break ties with Mr. Fawcett, and I didn't want to lose his friendship. Just the thought of not being able to see Thomas made my heart ache. But I knew the moment Emily was reprimanded or punished, she would gossip about the budding friendship between me and Thomas, of which dad had no inkling.

Nineteen

The air pressure that morning was bothering me. The air felt heavy and suffocating. Breathing was somewhat difficult for me. Perhaps this was heightened by the fear of joining Thomas on this crazy adventure.

When we arrived at Cloudesley Square, he dismissed his carriage, not wanting to draw any attention to us. We stood in front of the church located in the center of the square. A hexagonal garden with railings surrounded the entire Holy Trinity Church. Some scaffolding on its side, facing beautiful stained-glass windows, indicated that the church must have been closed for maintenance. It was early, and there was no movement around it.

We spent some time observing Mrs. Gertie Holyhead's house. It was a corner house, with the side facing one of the four entrances to the square. The ground floor had arched windows, and the two upper floors had square windows set back within an arch, all of which were closed. Five steps led to the main entrance, which had a wrought iron balcony. We didn't notice any movement inside.

We approached the side of the house. It was a wall of yellow and brown bricks, with just one window on the ground floor. Thomas forced the window and felt it give way. We heard footsteps heading towards the main door.

"It's crazy trying to break into this house in broad daylight," I whispered anxiously, as Thomas moved away from the window.

The door opened. A short, sturdy man with a red pepper-like nose dressed in time-worn clothes looked our way. Before he could react, Thomas asked:

"Good morning. Is this Mr. Lyonel Ward's residence?"

The man was taken aback.

"No. That gentleman doesn't live here," he said while locking the door and then descending the steps.

"Sorry, I'm from The Express newspaper, and our editor sent us here for an interview with Mr. Ward."

"No one lives here. I'm the watchman. You've got the wrong address. Good day."

The man passed us heading for the street next to his house, glancing at the window. Did he see Thomas messing with it? As he walked, he looked back at us heading to the church and then continued on his way.

"You're right, it's better we return at night. Why would someone guard an empty house?" Thomas questioned, as we walked toward Liverpool Road in search of a rental carriage.

"I have no idea. There's something about that house that scares me. Maybe you're right, the house must not be completely empty - Lyonel Ward, what kind of name is that?"

"I looked it up. It's the name of the previous owner of the house."

"Who's the current owner?"

"I couldn't find out."

That night, the iron gate didn't creak. The flickering lights of the square's lanterns and the fog covering Gordon Square played into my madness. They covered me like a dark gray cloak and made my slight escape unnoticed. Thomas was waiting for me in his carriage, having covered the family crest imprinted on the door. He gave orders to his coachman, Wilkes, and we headed for Cloudesley Square.

The moon, though hidden among the clouds, was the sole witness of our arrival at the square. We stayed inside the carriage next to the church, watching the house. It seemed more sinister at night. I imagined a thousand things that could have happened inside. Its windows were asleep but ready to wake up with incandescent eyes the moment we broke in. Thomas was mad, and I was even madder for joining him on this insane adventure at this hour of the night.

"Let's go, Thomas, we can't wait any longer."

I got out of the vehicle. I was wearing a light and black dress to facilitate my movements and help blend into the night. Thomas directed Wilkes to stop at one of the square's entrances and keep an eye out for any suspicious movements.

We approached the side window of the house, which Thomas had forced open earlier that morning. We heard no noise from inside the room. Thomas had brought a small iron bar, with which he forced the window open. He opened it slowly, praying it wouldn't squeak. He easily jumped over the sill and entered. Inside, I could see nothing; the thick velvet curtain was in the way. It was a nerve-wracking few seconds of waiting, I looked around to see if anyone or any neighbors were spying on us. No one.

Thomas reappeared to help me in, despite my light dress, the window was high. I couldn't climb up alone.

"I'll pull you up, try to give yourself a boost and sit on the sill," he whispered.

Just then, we heard the distant sound of a guard's whistle, getting closer. I raised my arms and jumped towards Thomas, who pulled me up with too much force, and as I sat on the sill, I lost my balance, falling onto Thomas and tangling in the curtain, which muffled the noise of our fall.

"What an interesting position you've gotten us into, Rowena," Thomas whispered in my ear.

Embarrassment showed on my face; my cheeks were burning red. I pushed Thomas to the side. I got up as quickly as I could, collected myself, and closed the window before the guard saw it open. I pulled the curtains, cutting us off from the outside world. A sliver of light from a lantern in the square entered through another window, also with thick curtains that were not fully closed.

The dim light that penetrated the room allowed us to notice that the living room was empty. There was no furniture, only an unlit fireplace, begging someone to bring it back to life. I swallowed hard, feeling fear start to nip at my back. We carefully explored the other rooms. No furniture. No signs of life. Thomas carried candles and Lucifer matches in his hands, but we avoided lighting them, fearing they would give our presence away. We came to a crossroads at the foot of the staircase. Go up to check the upper floors, or down to the basement? We decided to head to the basement, which would be the most logical place to hide the boy, Bob.

We opened the door leading to the basement. Complete darkness. We descended the stairs step by step, cautious not to fall, as we couldn't see anything. I placed my hand on Thomas's back, who insisted on not lighting the candles. We reached the bottom of the stairs. Darkness had enveloped us. Not a single ray of light entered the basement; if there were any windows, they were surely well sealed. We stopped for a while at the foot of the stairs, trying to hear any sign of breathing in the environment.

"I need to light the candle; we can't examine this place without some light," Thomas whispered.

The light temporarily blinded me when the Lucifer match was struck and then the candle. The light from the wick illuminated a small circle around us. Even with the limited light, we noticed that the basement had small windows, covered with thick curtains. They did not allow light to infiltrate the space. The walls were brick covered with stucco, the floor was laid with rough concrete. Thomas held the candle as high as he could while I followed closely behind, holding onto his arm. As we reached the central part of the basement, I began to smell a sweet and nauseating odor. The smell of a corpse. Despite the scarce light emanating from the candle, I could see a large circle, with a five-pointed star drawn on the ground.

"My God, it's a pentagram!" I gripped Thomas's arm tightly, as terror chilled my veins. My legs weakened. He turned and embraced me in his arms.

"Calm down, Rowena, they must be using this place for some ritual."

We continued walking arm in arm towards the end of the basement. An altar, which I couldn't make out clearly, with a long table in front stained with reddish marks, emerged from the darkness. My heart raced erratically. A slight noise from the direction of the stairs snapped us out of the inertia that had taken over. We turned with a speed I didn't know we possessed. Thomas held the candle in one hand, and in the other the iron bar with which he had opened the window. The light from the candle was not sufficient to reach the stairs. We walked apprehensively towards it. I felt my courage sink to my toes, and I believe Thomas's did too, as there was a slight tremor in the hand holding the candle. Upon reaching the stairs, I noticed a door beneath them. We approached it cautiously, hearing faint noises coming from the room inside. I didn't have the courage to open the door. Thomas grasped the doorknob and turned it very slowly while also peering in with the candle and his face through the opening that formed. Then I saw him, little Bob, bound and gagged, thrown in the corner of a dirty floor. I held the candle so Thomas could untie Bob and remove his gag.

"Sorry, Mr. Thomas. They caught me."

Thomas hugged the boy, giving him pats on the back as a gesture of comfort to calm him down.

"Let's get out of here before we become prisoners too," Thomas said.

They got up and left the room.

"You can tell me what happened later," said Thomas.

We climbed the stairs as fast as we could. Upon reaching the living room, we went to the window by our entrance. Three whistle blows pierced through the night just as Thomas was opening the window.

"Damn, the guard!" I exclaimed.

"No. Someone's coming. It's Wilkes warning us."

A key began to turn in the lock of the door where we were. Bob snatched the iron bar from Thomas's hands and ran towards the entrance.

"Jump out the window, I'll be right behind you," said Bob, ducking behind the door.

The door opened just as I was sitting on the inner sill of the window. The guard looked at us in amazement, and three things happened at that exact moment. Bob struck the man who had entered with all his might in the shin with the iron bar. Thomas pushed me, and soon after, he jumped out the window himself.

The window was a bit high, but the dress softened my fall. Shocked by the shove, I confess I didn't land like a lady. I ended up scraping my elbow and hand on the street's stones. Thomas landed beside me, like a cat. He quickly got up, helping me to my feet. My wounds began to heal. We ran towards our carriage, where Wilkes waited with the door open. Bob shook off the guard and ran towards us. We quickly climbed into the carriage and took our seats. My chest was heaving. Bob threw himself into the vehicle, which took off with the door still open. Thomas closed it, and I looked out the window of the carriage. The guard screamed and waved his fists in our direction. Whether he could identify us in the dim light with the moon still hidden among the clouds was unclear. But in any case, he knew a couple had rescued the boy.

"What happened with the guard, Bob?" I asked.

"I hit him with the iron bar in his shin, and he fell to the ground screaming in pain. I took the chance with the door open and fled. It was he who caught me. I was watching the house when I saw a carriage arrive. A well-dressed gentleman got out, and as soon as he entered, I went to one of the windows to see if I could find out anything. Someone put a wet cloth on my face, and I passed out."

"Chloroform," I said.

"When I woke up, I was tied up and thrown in the corner of a large room on the upper part of the house, with tables full of test tubes, a microscope, and glass things, looking like a laboratory. This gentleman I had seen entering was scolding the guard, showing he didn't like him bringing me into the house at all. He ordered the guard to lock me in a small basement room, where you found me. Later, he would decide what to do with me. By his anger, I think they were planning to kill me."

"Did you happen to hear the name of this man, or what he was doing in the house?" Thomas inquired.

"No, the guard didn't mention his name in my presence, but those things in the basement indicate they are up to no good there."

"Did you get to see the altar at the back of the basement?"

"I did, but very quickly. The guard locked me up right away, and it was poorly lit down there. I couldn't see the details. I'm sorry, Mr. Thomas."

"It's alright, Bob. The important thing is that you're safe," Thomas said, placing a generous coin in Bob's hand. "Now you need to eat and rest. I'll take you to your home."

Only a few hours had passed since I had snuck out of the house. Everyone was still asleep. I opened the door with a spare key... that even Max didn't know I had. My wounds on the hand and elbow had disappeared, leaving no mark of my adventure. Just a light dirt from the ground where I had fallen. And it, by the way, was no longer on my body after the bath I took.

Lying in bed, I reflected on the tumultuous and reckless night. My outings were becoming increasingly dangerous. I tried to prevent Thomas from doing something foolish, and ended up getting involved in a risky and insane situation. But, most importantly, we managed to save Bob. I shudder to think what they would have done to the boy. Thomas, on our way back, mentioned something significant. That house was the link to the murdered young women. A cloud of sinister thoughts enveloped me, and I eventually fell asleep.

Twenty

It was one of those mornings I wished I hadn't woken up. A feeling of guilt overwhelmed me. I had been sneaking around and acting behind my father's back in a rather irresponsible manner. Slipping out into the night for adventures that no other girl my age would even dream of, not even in their worst nightmares. The emotional turmoil I experienced the night before made me reflect. Was I doing the right thing? Wouldn't it be more appropriate to tell my father what I had discovered, and he, in his way, could relay it to Inspector Tennyson?

I was emotionally drained; my entire body felt the stress. These weren't physical pains, but rather in the soul. I was fragile, my mind exhausted, and my stomach was screaming, "I'm starving."

I headed down to the tea room, when the angry voice of my father, coming from the library, caught my attention. I entered the library to find my father sitting there, tense, newspaper in hand, and Emily gesturing wildly.

"What happened, dad?"

"It's your sister. She can't stop asking for new clothes," my dad explained nervously, in a way I had never seen before. "She thinks I'm some high-ranking bank official, or even the banker himself."

"It's just one more dress, dad. Just one. It's a beautiful model, I've even taken the measurements, it should be almost ready," said Emily.

"Emily, it's been a short while since we got some new dresses. I don't see the need for more clothes. Be understanding," I said, trying to calm my sister down.

"Stay out of this, Rowena."

"Emily, lower your voice. Your sister is absolutely right. I can't afford new dresses right now, and you don't need them at this moment."

"I hate you, Rowena, you'll pay for this," screamed Emily, standing up and leaving the library.

"Emily, come back here. Emily!" shouted dad. But my sister, ran up the stairs and slammed her room door.

"Your sister needs a good lesson. She's becoming very disobedient. I know I'm to blame for Emily's behavior. I've often turned a blind eye to her defiance, trying to make up for the mother she misses. But I see now that I've made mistakes in her upbringing, and I can't manage it any longer," he said with remorse.

"No, dad. I believe Emily's very essence is to be rebellious and dissatisfied with everything and everyone. Of course, the presence of a strong maternal figure would have helped. You should have remarried."

"Do you miss your mother?"

"The few memories I have of her, I still hold dear. I also miss having a female presence in our home. I believe Emily does too. That's why she's so rebellious. So many things could have been done; outings, trips, shopping... Many pieces of advice about life she could have given us. And most of all, a bit of maternal love."

"My God! How unfair I've been. I locked my pain away just for myself. And forgot that you also suffered. I should have opened my heart again to life. Maybe you would have been happier."

"But I am happy," I said, holding my father's hand between mine and tenderly caressing it.

"I tried, Rowena, to give you a second mother. But my feelings for Charity, are still deeply ingrained in my heart. I've even had hallucinations about her."

"Hallucinations... what do you mean, dad?"

"Sometimes in the dead of night, I wake up startled and see her sitting on the sofa, looking at me. Ahh... Rowena, it seems so real."

My father's mood had changed so quickly. From the anger he felt, to a deep melancholy. Dr. Robert was not well. This rapid shift in mood was not one of his characteristics. He had always been a grounded man.

"How long have you had these visions?"

"For a short while, but don't worry about me, I'm fine. You haven't had your breakfast yet. You must be starving."

"I'm sorry, dad, you're not fine."

I felt an overwhelming desire to open up to my father. To tell him all about my discoveries, my burgeoning feelings for Thomas, and the dangers we've faced together. But today was not the moment, he was already weakened by his memories and had been upset enough with Emily. I let go of his hand and went to have breakfast.

"Rowena, later tell your sister she can make the dress. But it will be the last one of this year. And you are the one to pick it up. I don't want her at the dressmaker's so soon. Emily is too easily influenced."

"I had my coffee, it went down bitter. I didn't enjoy the breakfast, despite the delicious cookies, cakes, and bread rolls right in front of me. I swallowed it more out of physiological need, as my stomach was screaming with hunger. But my thoughts were elsewhere."

Emily's room door was locked. I knocked softly, but there was no answer.

"Emily, please open the door."

"Leave me alone."

"I have news about your dress - there was silence for a few seconds from the other side of the door. Then the key turned."

"Come in...quickly."

The bedroom's fireplace was still crackling, with the last embers glowing from the night. Emily leaned back on the bed, where a damp handkerchief was carelessly thrown. Her eyes were still moist, and her cheeks were red from crying. I sat on the leather sofa near the fireplace.

"What do you want to talk to me about?"

"It's about the dress. Dad gave permission to make it. But he said it's the last one this year."

"Of course. I promise it will be the last."

"You need to pay more attention to Dad. His emotions aren't well. And stop worrying about trivialities."

"He seemed fine to me this morning, a bit more irritable, but okay."

"That's the irritability I'm talking about. It's not like him. Something is stressing him out. We need to be alert - I stood up to leave the room. - Another thing, he asked me to pick up the dress when it's ready. He doesn't want you at the dressmaker's again this year."

Emily frowned, and I left the room, heading towards the library.

My father was no longer in the library, his newspaper was tossed on the armchair. Worried, I called Max.

"Doctor Robert went to visit a patient," he said.

I picked up the newspaper from the couch, flipped through it randomly, not focusing on any page, carefully folded it and placed it on the table. I walked over to the shelf and looked for the pharmaceutical catalog. I searched for the information I had glanced at the other day about the blue pills.

The pills were mercury-based, slowly poisoning the patient, causing various side effects; such as irritation and hallucinations. And in the final stage, madness. That's why my father's mood was changing. And he was having hallucinations of Mom. What grave disease did he have to be taking these cursed pills for? I flipped the page and then discovered that the mercury pills were prescribed for gout, kidney stones, but mainly for Syphilis.

My hands turned cold, powerless, and the catalog fell from my hands straight to the floor. My God! My father had syphilis. I searched the library books for one about the disease. I picked up the catalog from the floor and with the volume I found on the shelf, I sat down. The disease has three stages. My father must be in the initial stage of the first; he showed no visible sores on his body, but he had an incurable disease.

I leaned my head back in the armchair and tried to process what I had read about the disease. The images I had seen in the book were shocking. Lost in thought, I heard Max talking with my father in the vestibule. Doctor Robert had returned.

I put the book back on the shelf, keeping only the pharmaceutical catalog. I waited for a while until he settled down and relaxed in his office. I knocked on the door and peeked into his study.

"Excuse me, may I come in?"

My father was writing and gestured for me to sit on the sofa in front of him.

"What is that in your hands?" he asked, pointing to the catalog.

I opened the book on the page I had marked, and placed it on the table. He looked at the text and then at me.

"I don't understand, Rowena."

"Forgive me for taking this liberty, dad. I saw you taking these blue pills, and I researched."

"But you shouldn't have. This is a subject that a young woman your age should neither know of nor take an interest in."

"I know it's a delicate and private issue. But I was worried about your health, and you're my father, not a stranger. And you also know I'm curious about medicine. This is a cursed disease. These pills could drive you mad and poison you."

"I had them made with a very low percentage of mercury. I don't have any symptoms of the disease yet. I don't even know if I have it. I'm just taking precautions."

"With a deadly pill? The side effects are starting to show, like your irritability today, the hallucinations with Mom. Is it worth taking a medicine for a disease you don't even know if you have? I'm sorry, dad. Who do you think you got it from?"

"From... actress Janet Darville."

"Was that the reason for the separation?"

"Yes, her contamination was a sign that she was unfaithful to me. That's why I started taking the pills."

"Do you have any symptoms?"

"No."

"Then stop taking those damned pills before you go mad."

"I promise I'll think about all of this. And let's not speak of it anymore, and don't mention anything to your sister. Now leave me alone. I have some letters to write."

"Yes, dad."

Twenty-One

I retreated to my room, looking to divert my thoughts. Aunt Annie had sent me a beautiful print from Paris as soon as she arrived in France. With the chaos of the last few days, I hadn't found the time to reply. I sat near the window where I could gaze upon the garden and the majestic trees of Gordon Square. My mind wandered, searching for the perfect words to pen Auntie's letter, when I noticed an individual leaning against one of the square's lampposts, very close to our house. He seemed to be staring in the direction of my window. I stood to get a better look. As our eyes met, my heart raced even though I didn't recognize him, something about him reminded me of the assassin of the actress Janet Darville. I froze. He averted his gaze, walked towards a nearby carriage, stepped in, and left.

I don't know how long I stood there, staring into the void. I was being watched, but by whom?

I refuse to believe it was a mere coincidence, that man standing there just when I looked through the window. He must have been observing me, waiting for some confirmation. If his intentions were not malicious, he wouldn't have left as soon as he realized I saw him.

I abandoned the letter I was writing to Aunt Anne. At that moment, I couldn't focus on composing beautiful words for her.

I don't know if recent events with my father have made me more vulnerable and fearful. I didn't feel safe with that man spying on us. My imagination might have been running wild. Perhaps the individual was there by chance, and our exchange of glances nothing but a fluke, but I was not at ease with the situation.

I descended the stairs and went to the street in front of our house. I positioned myself next to the post, in the same spot and manner as the intruder had been. My eyes fell on the windows of my room. There was no doubt; he had been watching me. For how long had I been under observation?

Two days later, Emily received a message from the dressmaker. Her dress was ready.

The afternoon was overshadowed by dark, heavy clouds, a looming sign of the imminent downpour.

I spent more time than I intended at the dressmaker's. She took too long making the final touches on Emily's dress. My sister had insisted on coming with me, but I blindly obeyed father's orders. Emily couldn't visit the seamstress any time soon.

Max, upon opening the door, took the box with the dress from my hands as I walked in.

"Is Emily in her room?" I asked, making my way to the living room.

"Miss Emily went out."

"Went out? But she was eager to see her new dress."

Max handed me a note.

"I received this message for you, Miss Emily, she read it and then left shortly after."

I opened the note with trembling hands, bracing for the worst.

I'm waiting for you, dear. At Cloudesley Square 18.

Urgent

T.

I sat on the sofa in disbelief. Could Emily have thought the message was from Thomas? And that he was arranging a secret rendezvous? Did she hope to catch us in the act, thinking this address was some clandestine love nest? Emily, your naivety and recklessness have put you in danger.

Thomas would never use "dear" something so intimate, in a message that could fall into anyone's hands, especially my father's. The note was a trap for me, and my sister ended up being the victim.

The rain outside started to pour heavily. The boom of a very close thunder, followed by the flash of its lightning, illuminated my face. I got scared. My sister was in danger.

I wrote a message to Thomas, briefly summarizing the situation. I called Max and handed him the note, sealed. I asked him to deliver it urgently and for the messenger to wait for a response.

"Miss, it's pouring rain, it wouldn't be wise for the messenger to leave now."

"Max, I'm sorry, but he must go now. Emily is in danger."

Max looked at me astounded, while I went up to Emily's room. I left the box with the dress on her bed and went to my quarters to change.

While waiting for the note's reply, I chose a very light dress to facilitate my movements. I looked for a hat with wide brims and as simple as possible; its purpose was to protect me from the rain, not to beautify me. I secured it in my hair with my long and sharp metal pins, which were my weapons. I grabbed a thick fabric overcoat to shelter myself from the rain, an umbrella, and went down to the library.

The rain had lessened in intensity, but lightning and thunder continued to crackle and light up the sky.

I asked Max to prepare me a warm and soothing tea. I needed to stay as relaxed as possible; it wasn't the time for a meltdown. The drink would give a false comfort to my stomach, which was already throwing bile up my throat.

Luckily, my father hadn't arrived yet. The rain must have held him back at the hospital. The last thing I needed at the moment was dad's intervention.

The warmth of the tea eased my anxieties. I heard Max answering the door. Finally, Thomas arrived. Max escorted him to the library, we looked at each other. No words needed to be said. He knew how I felt. I extended my hands to him, and he pulled me toward him, hugging me tightly. Despite being damp from the rain, I felt the warmth of his embrace — and a bulge at his waist. It was a pistol.

"Everything will be okay, Rowena. Can we go?"

"Yes, I'm ready."

Max handed Thomas his damp overcoat in the vestibule. He put it on, raised the collar, and we stepped out into the rain.

We ran to his carriage. He placed a blanket over my legs. And we set off.

Outside, the rain was relentless, with lightning slicing the sky like blazing arrows, seemingly about to split the carriage in half. I held hands with Thomas for much of the journey. We didn't speak for a long time, only our rapid breathing could be heard inside the carriage.

Wilkes, the coachman, despite being outside and enduring the harsh weather, performed his job impeccably, avoiding large puddles that could hide potholes, and other carriages that were driving recklessly due to the storm.

At one point, water splashed from the wheels of another vehicle, hitting our window hard, bringing us back to reality.

"Do you have any plan, Thomas?"

"No! I'm going on instinct."

"I'm really scared."

"Me too, that's why I brought a weapon. And I asked Wilkes to come armed."

"Do you think my sister is okay?"

"I believe so. To them, Emily is just a hostage. They'll keep her alive, stay calm. They want you."

"Thomas, please, how can I stay calm with my neck on the line."

Twenty-Two

The first sign of nightfall enveloped us as soon as we arrived at Cloudesley Square. The ceaseless rain and the furious lightning streaking across the sky made our hearts race with fear. Wilkes stopped right in front of number 18, where we suspected Emily was being held captive. The darkness prevailed inside the house, raising our suspicions. Not a single light was to be seen. Wilkes stepped down from the carriage, shielded by his thick raincoat, and approached the door, trying to force it open. To his surprise, the door was unlocked. Wilkes drew his weapon, and we stepped out of the carriage. Thomas also grabbed his pistol, and we entered the house, with Wilkes keeping watch at the entrance.

The interior of the house remained as it was during our last visit. Not a single piece of furniture. I ran my fingers through the ashes in the fireplace. Cold. Nothing had changed since our last visit.

Thomas lit a candle from a candelabra, which rested on the fireplace, and we went down to the basement. I held the candelabra, and Thomas his weapon. Not a soul in sight, especially not in the basement. In the small room under the stairs, no sign of my sister. I cast the candelabra's light toward where the altar stood. Nothing. The basement was empty, as if it had never been used. Even the pentagram that had been drawn on the floor was erased without leaving a trace of its existence.

Thomas and I exchanged puzzled looks. What was going on in this house? I remembered that Bob had mentioned a chemical laboratory upstairs.

We went to the second floor. All the rooms were empty, not a piece of furniture in sight. In one of the rooms, two test tubes lay on the floor, indicating that this was indeed the laboratory Bob Little had seen.

We went downstairs and found Wilkes still with his pistol drawn, and then we left the house.

"Thomas, the things we saw in this house, they're gone. It's like waking up from a nightmare. Where could my sister be?"

The rain showed no signs of stopping. The lightning continued to slash the sky.

A violent thunderclap unleashed a tremendous burst of electricity. The bolt struck the church tower and branched out to the tips of the wrought-iron fence encircling the entire building. The flash was so intense it lit up the square. Startled, I shielded my head with my hands, looking toward the tower where the lightning had struck. That's when I noticed a light inside, and the main door of the church was ajar.

The scaffolding remained in place. A sign that the construction was not yet completed. Could someone have broken into the church?

"Look how odd, Thomas! There's someone in the church tower."

"Shouldn't it be closed for renovation?" questioned Thomas.

We ran to the gate. Thomas took the lead and opened it. The moment he touched the iron gate, he was thrown to the ground with such force it was as if he had been kicked by a mule. It was the result of the electrical charge accumulated in the fence when the lightning struck it.

Dazed from the shock, Thomas remained on the ground, the rain pouring down on him. Wilkes rushed over to help me lift him.

"Are you alright, Thomas?" I asked, concerned.

"I'm a bit dizzy. My gloves lessened the shock, could've been a lot worse."

I heard a muffled scream that seemed to come from the direction of the tower. Chilled to the bone, could it be Emily? I asked Wilkes to stay with Thomas as he recovered, and I entered through the gate left open by Thomas's fall. He yelled for me to wait, but I couldn't hear anything, so overwhelmed was I by the fear clutching at my heart. There was no time to wait for his recovery. My sister needed my help.

I pushed open the partially open door of the church and went inside. No one there. Only the light from the lightning entering through the stained-glass windows. The rainbow of colors that filtered into the church would have been worth admiring at any other time, but not now. I found the staircase behind the sacristy leading to the tower. A faint light from its top dimly illuminated the steps, but still, I ascended as quickly as I could. Fear sped up my heartbeat, and recklessness overtook me. I wanted nothing more than to save my sister.

The thunder outside continued to batter my ears, making my chest and my breathing jerk more than ever. I reached the tower, and candles lit a grotesque chemical laboratory set upon an improvised table. Behind it, leaning against one of the long stained-glass windows, was a repulsive figure with unkempt hair like a madman and bloodshot eyes, holding Emily hostage. One hand covered her mouth, while the other held a knife to her throat. Despite his disheveled clothes, they were of fine quality, and I could see the silver cufflinks adorned with a precious stone.

I heard footsteps climbing, and turning around, I saw Thomas pointing a gun at the madman who had kidnapped my sister.

"George Holyhead, why did you kidnap my sister?"

"The message I sent was for you. This lunatic showed up in your place. Screaming and looking for Thomas."

"Mr. Holyhead, we barely know each other. Why do you want to make me your prisoner?" I asked, trying to remain as calm as possible.

"I want your blood. The power of your blood. I'm very sick. I was on a medical mission a year ago in Kolkata, and to my misfortune, I contracted malaria in its most aggressive form. I was between life and death with serious sequelae. In addition to the fever, I have migraines that leave me utterly distraught from the intense headache and severe eye pain, for days on end. I tried various treatments, even the most radical, but the intervals between the attacks are decreasing and becoming stronger. I don't want to go mad. I need your blood to cleanse my body of this cursed malaria."

"My blood? How do you know it has this healing power?"

Emily struggled in his arms while he spewed his tortured words at me. Thomas, by my side, nervous, continued to point the gun. Lightning and thunder outside gave no respite. My God! What a hellish night.

"A few months ago, I found Dr. Victor's diary, along with some letters in my father's belongings. Including a newspaper clipping about the birth of Frankenstein's daughter. I asked various questions and found out that Dr. Robert had brought the mother and baby to London. All I had to do was follow him."

"So that's why you killed all those young women, who, unfortunately for them, had a birthmark as described in the newspaper and were about the right age. And somehow, they were linked to my father. You thought one of them was the creature's daughter."

My sister's eyes widened when I mentioned "the creature's daughter," and I felt Thomas's hand tremble with the gun.

"In my pain's desperation, I failed to think logically, that was my mistake. Only did I discover it was you when you decided to rescue that nosy boy from my house, right in the square. My lookout mentioned it was the same couple who identified themselves as journalists from The Express that morning. Then I remembered Thomas was from the newspaper, and you were at the party with him at my house, and you were Dr. Robert's daughter, and guess what, you were 16."

"But then why all those ritual marks in the basement of the house, if in reality you wanted my blood?"

The conversation Emily was hearing made her nervous and scared, making abrupt movements to free herself. George started to grow impatient. I grabbed Thomas's arm, holding the gun as a sign for him to wait. I feared that in his madness, George would stab Emily.

"I sought out radical treatments; black magic rituals were one of them. But they left me more tormented. Until my mother found out during her visit and forced me to put an end to everything. After you discovered the house, I came to this tower. Here, no one bothers me, not even the vicar. A generous donation shut him up."

"George, let Emily go. I'm an excellent shooter."

"You're an idiot, Thomas, that's what you are. Put down the gun on the table. Now! Or she dies."

I looked at Thomas and nodded. Thomas approached the table, laid the gun upon it, and returned to my side.

A mighty thunderclap exploded above us, and lightning struck the church tower with all its might, sparking over the stained glass, catching us off guard. George relaxed his grip on Emily's body. Then she bit his hand, managing to free herself and ran towards me, I hugged her with all the strength my emotions allowed.

George recovered from the shock, advanced towards the table, and grabbed the pistol Thomas had left, pointing it in my direction. Insanely, he spoke:

"I will kill you and have your blood one way or another," and he pulled the trigger.

"No!" Emily screamed, throwing her body in front of mine, placing herself between me and the bullet.

The shot hit my sister, in the stomach, the impact throwing her to the ground. Before George could shoot again, Thomas jumped on him. Their bodies collided and fell through one of the tower's stained-glass windows, plunging into the sky.

A scream of despair erupted from within me; my sister was wounded, lying on the ground, and Thomas was dead. I ran to the window and saw Thomas lying still, on one of the scaffolding planks near the window. Below, George's lifeless body on another wooden platform.

I raced back to help my sister, who was bleeding and agonizing from the gunshot.

"I don't want to die, Rowena. I'm still so young."

"You're not going to die, please don't move and do exactly as I say."

I carefully removed the coat Emily was wearing. I opened her shirt slightly to get a better look at her wound. It was bleeding heavily. I tore the sleeve off her dress and placed it over the wound, asking Emily to press down hard to try to reduce the bleeding. I went to the laboratory table and found a device used for transfusion. It was probably something George intended to use on me. It was a small cylindrical glass reservoir, with a round metal base and a valve to control the blood flow, from which two sheep's guts protruded, one for the donor and the other for the receiver. They had small metal cannulas with needles attached at their ends. One of the guts was divided into two parts, connected by a small balloon-shaped pump, to help pump blood into the patient.

My sister moaned in pain lying on the floor, and without a second thought, I took the device and explained to Emily what I was going to do. It might hurt a bit, but she had to trust me. I asked her to let go of the cloth over her wound and hold the glass reservoir over her body, without tilting it. Using a sheep's gut, I found thrown on the table, I made a small tourniquet around my arm to aid the exit of my blood. I inserted one of the needles into the vein in my forearm. It hurt a bit; the needle was quite thick. And then I slowly inserted the other needle, attached to the gut with the balloon pump, into Emily's forearm vein. She moaned as the needle went in. I sat next to her keeping her lying down to facilitate the reception of my blood, which began to appear in the glass reservoir. I let a bit more blood accumulate, then opened the metal valve as little as possible, slowly releasing my blood into Emily.

"Emily, you're not going to die, not even if I have to drain all the blood from my body."

I waited a few seconds for the blood to flow through the gut and gently squeezed the balloon pump a few times. My blood gained strength and began to feed Emily's arm. I don't know how long we were there; the process was slow, and Emily eventually fell asleep, and I ended up having to hold the reservoir she had let go of.

Alone in my thoughts, worried whether Thomas had survived the impact of the fall on the scaffolding. And George, what madness. What was his condition? I examined Emily's wound; it had stopped bleeding. A good sign, my blood was taking effect in her body. It was time to wake her up and remove the needles from our arms. The blood I had donated was enough. I tapped her face gently. She woke up.

"It's time for us to go home, and you need to rest."

"I stopped bleeding!" she said, astonished, placing her hand over the wound. "Your blood really is magical as George said, that's why he was so desperate. Are you really adopted?"

"Dad will explain everything, now it's time for us to leave. You need to rest."

I removed the needle from my arm and then from Emily's. I pressed the tip of her shirt against the hole in her arm for a few seconds, and the blood stopped. On my forearm, there was only a sign of clotted blood that came out when I removed the needle. Not even a mark of the needle hole remained.

Rapid footsteps ascending the tower stairs startled us. Was it George returning? Three people entered: first my father, then Inspector Tennyson, and lastly, soaking wet, Thomas. My heart raced, I quickly stood up and ran to Thomas, wrapping him in my arms and hugging him tightly. He moaned, the fall had hurt him. Then I let him go.

"I thought you were dead!"

Dad knelt next to Emily, examined her wound, picked up the device I had used for the transfusion off the ground, and saw blood still inside it. He looked at me and understood everything. No words were spoken, as the inspector was present.

"And George, is he dead?" I asked anxiously.

"He escaped. As soon as he recovered from the fall, he climbed down the scaffolding. Wilkes told me he even shot at him but missed. Then he helped me down, I was still very dizzy. A bit later your father arrived with the inspector, and I explained everything to them."

"How did you get here, dad?" Emily asked.

"Max showed me the message that your sister had received and mentioned that Rowena told him you were in danger. I summoned the inspector, who promptly joined me."

"I need to know in detail what happened here," said the inspector.

"Not now, inspector. We can talk later. At the moment, your job is to search for and arrest Mr. George Holyhead, for the kidnapping and attempted murder of my daughters, and as Thomas has also informed you, for the murder of the other girls."

Dad helped Emily to stand up and very slowly descended the stairs, providing support for her.

I said goodbye to Thomas and of course to Wilkes, who gave the inspector a lift, since he had come in my father's carriage. I settled Emily lying down on one of the seats of our carriage, and my father and I sat on the other.

"Thomas, I would like you to come to our house early tomorrow morning. We need to clear up everything that happened. Now go and rest."

"Yes, Dr. Robert."

Anxious, Max opened the door and asked my father for permission to carry Emily in his arms up the stairs to her room. I took off my damp overcoat and handed it to Lucy. I asked her to prepare a nice bath for me and for Emily, as we were covered in grime.

I advised Dad that there was no need for him to stitch the gunshot wound, unless he wanted to remove the bullet from Emily's body. I had had a similar experience with Thomas, and he was left with no scar.

"Does Thomas know about the secret of your blood?"

"Sorry, Dad. It happened on the night of the Holyhead's ball. He was stabbed in the arm while trying to save me from the villain. And Emily found out everything from Mr. George."

"It seems we have a lot to discuss tomorrow with Thomas. Now I'm going to see how your sister is doing and talk with her."

Twenty-three

I woke up early, unable to get a good night's sleep. Lucy came in and opened the curtains. The sky was clear, no sign of last night's storm.

"Has Emily woken up? Is she alright?"

"Yes, Miss Emily even had her breakfast. Dr. Robert was giving her some medicine."

"Please bring my coffee while I get dressed."

I had my breakfast, while Lucy tidied up my hair, and then I went to my sister's room. I wasn't sure how I'd be received by her, after George's revelations.

"Hey! How's my sick girl doing?" I said affectionately.

"Good! Sit here beside me, on the edge of the bed."

"Did you have a fever? Did dad put on a bandage?"

"No fever. Dad said it's almost healed. I asked him to leave the bullet in if it wouldn't cause any complications. It didn't hit any vital organs."

"Nothing's going to happen to you, my blood in you will protect against any infection from the bullet."

"Dad told me everything. Why didn't you tell me about your special blood and that you were adopted?"

"I was afraid you wouldn't like me. You had your own worries. And I only found out I was adopted recently. Why did you jump in front of the bullet?"

"You went there to save me. To give your life for mine. You knew he wanted your blood, that he was a killer, yet you went. I could see how much you loved me. I couldn't let you die."

I hugged Emily in bed and kissed her forehead. The shooting had changed something in my sister's heart, and it seemed for the better.

Max appeared at the door to announce that Emily had a visitor, complaining that it was too early by any standard to receive anyone, but had nonetheless asked Mr. Crotch to wait in the living room. Emily and I exchanged looks and smiled; Joanna Fawcett's friend hadn't wasted any time.

"Max, bring Mr. Crotch to my room. Rowena will keep me company."

I placed an upholstered chair near Emily's bed. Mr. Edmund Crotch asked for permission and entered timidly. He greeted me and then Emily. He handed her a beautiful bouquet of wildflowers. I took the flowers from Emily and indicated the chair for him to sit. I placed the flowers in a vase on the table and sat down on the couch in front of the fireplace. We talked about various subjects and laughed at his stories. Emily was always gracious with Mr. Crotch, which impressed me. Upon leaving, he asked my permission to court Emily. I was embarrassed, knowing Emily had other interests, and it was dad who should give such permission.

"Sorry, Mr. Crotch, although I am the elder sister, it's Emily who has to decide if she would like to date you, and dad to give his permission."

I looked at Emily questioningly. She nodded and said:

"Mr. Crotch, I'd like to receive you for now as a friend. If you want to visit me under those conditions."

"Of course! Miss Emily. I'd be delighted."

Emily rang the bell, and Max accompanied Mr. Crotch out.

"I don't understand, you didn't want anything to do with him a short while ago."

"Mr. Crotch is elegant, a good man, comes from a good family and seems to like me a lot. Maybe I'll give him a chance."

"And Thomas?" I asked apprehensively.

"Thomas and you were made for each other. I was naive and with my fits of jealousy thought the world revolved around me. The trauma of the kidnapping and then the shooting, where I felt death close at hand, showed me that in reality, I'm no different from anyone else."

"Excuse me, Miss Stein, Dr. Robert is calling you to his office," Max said at the bedroom door.

"Uh oh! Trouble's brewing," said Emily.

I went downstairs apprehensively, having to reveal all the schemes and lies I had told my father. I knocked on the door and entered. My heart leaped. Thomas was sitting on the couch.

"Good morning, dad. Hello, Thomas."

"Sit down, Rowena. Thomas has already given me an overview of your adventures in London, and I must confess I didn't like what I heard."

I sat on the other couch next to Thomas and recounted to my father how everything started. The first murder, the concern over the birthmark, which led us to the morgue, the clues we uncovered, the chases, the stabbing of Thomas, the attempts on our lives, our presence at the death of actress Janet Darville, and the rescue of the boy Bob. I didn't mention Mary Penny's frivolity. My father was horrified, that all this happened right under his nose.

"Thomas, I've always trusted you. How could you expose Rowena to so much danger?"

"It wasn't his fault, dad. Since the first death, I felt the killer was after my blood. I was just trying to stay one step ahead. And Thomas helped me in this search. Unfortunately, things spiraled out of our control, and there was no turning back."

"You should have left this matter to the police. Inspector Tennyson, despite his brusqueness, is an excellent detective."

"I know. I thought about doing that many times. But I would have had to reveal my adoption, my bloodline, and that I am the daughter of a monster. And I didn't want to." I looked at Thomas, those last words hurt to say.

"Rowena, you didn't even trust me, your father, to share these findings."

"Remember the other day when we talked about the blue pills? I entered your office to tell you. But you were so distant and overwhelmed with problems, I gave up. I didn't want to add to your worries."

Max interrupted us, informing that Inspector Tennyson was waiting in the living room. Dad had him brought to the office and asked us to stay. The inspector might need some clarification.

"Good morning, Inspector. Any news about George?" I asked.

"Unfortunately, no. He's still missing. I visited the Holyhead' house last night and Dr. Henry is out of London. Mrs. Gertie mentioned she knew her son was ill, but not to this extent of madness. I mentioned the murders of the three girls, and actress Janet Darville. She was horrified. But she was emphatic in stating that her son didn't kill Miss Darville. I pressed her a bit more, and mentioned what Mr. Fawcett revealed to me about her last night.

"What did Thomas tell you?" I queried.

"That she was pretending to be disabled. She revealed, due to treatment with a holistic therapist for a year, she was cured. The intimacy of the massages turned them into lovers, but she discovered he was having an affair with actress Janet Darville. She decided to end everything. But he blackmailed her with hefty sums of money, threatening to reveal everything to her husband. She believes he killed the actress."

"Does Dr. Holyhead know she's cured?" Dad asked

"I don't think so. I feel she uses this disability pretense to keep herself from conjugal duties. But if he finds out, this marriage is over," said the inspector.

"Did she tell you who the blackmailer is?" Thomas asked.

"Yes. It's Micajah but known as Cage. He's a bad character, I don't know how such a distinguished lady fell for someone like him. I'm heading to his office now."

"Loneliness and vulnerability make us fragile, Inspector. Please, let me know if it was him who killed Janet Darville. I have a vested interest in this matter."

Max showed Mr. Tennyson out as we stood up to leave my father's office.

"Wait a minute, I'd like to clarify one more matter with you."

We sat down again, and I looked at Thomas with some worry. Could it be that after recent events, dad would forbid Thomas from visiting our home?

"Only someone with an emotional attachment to another would follow them through thick and thin. Thomas, are you and Rowena dating?"

Thomas's face blushed quickly, and my cheeks began to burn, they must have been crimson.

"No! Dr. Robert. We are just friends and I've respected her, but I have a great interest in your daughter. Rowena has not yet given me a chance to ask for your permission."

"Thomas, you rascal, throwing the ball in my court."

"You know that because of recent events, I ought to banish you from this house. But I know that much of the blame for all this lies with Rowena having influenced you. She, in the heat of her discoveries about being adopted, acted recklessly and you, to please her, fell into this diabolical web that George spun. I thank you for trying to protect my daughter in your way, even taking a stabbing and nearly dying from a fall yesterday. Now you know she is adopted and whose daughter she is. For the sake of our friendship, I wish this secret to die within these walls."

"Of course, Dr. Robert, I've always had respect and admiration for you, I would never betray your trust. Besides, I had already given my word to Rowena."

"Despite being two reckless young people, you make a handsome couple. I'm not sure if Rowena agrees with me."

"Yes, of course, dad," I said shyly.

"Thomas, would you like to visit Emily?" I asked, changing the subject.

"If your father doesn't mind?"

Dad nodded in agreement, and we quickly left the office, heading to Emily's room.

On our way to the room, I told Thomas that Emily, after the kidnapping, had changed for the better. She welcomed him warmly, but without the clinginess that dominated their previous encounters. She seemed happier, lighter; I don't know if the malice that once filled her being had dissipated along with the blood she lost when shot. God willing, I preferred the new Emily.

Twenty-Four

Two days had passed since the chaos at the tower. Emily had recovered, and at the site of the gunshot wound, there was only a faint mark indicating where the bullet had hit her, which would soon disappear. It was still sore, but not for much longer.

"The dress looks beautiful, Rowena, but I think the seamstress needs to take it in a bit here at the waist," said Emily, trying on the dress I had picked up for her for the first time.

"You're still recovering; you must have lost some weight. If she takes it in, it won't fit you anymore. I can ask Lucy to adjust it if you insist."

"Sorry, Rowena, nothing against our Lucy, but this dress was expensive. The seamstress should be obliged to make the adjustments I need."

"Mark how much you want the dress to be taken in. I'll visit her later and will wait for her to make the necessary adjustments. I'll take Lucy with me; with George still on the loose, I dare not go out alone."

The police hadn't found George. He remained at large. The inspector had arrested the therapist Cage as soon as he left my father's office.

According to Mr. Tennyson's account to my father. Under pressure from the police, Cage confessed that he had killed his lover, the actress Janet Darville, over a despicable reason. She had told him about her pregnancy, and Cage demanded Ms. Darville get an abortion. They argued, and in the heat of the moment, rage got the better of him, and without thinking, he strangled the actress. By the time he realized, she was dead. Desperate not to be incriminated, he remembered the murders of the young girls, then slit Ms. Darville's throat, attempting to mislead the police.

But then we showed up. And he almost slashed my throat too. What a horrific creature, that Cage! That's why he had been watching my window, thinking I had recognized him. But how did he know where I lived?

Poor Dad was devastated by the Inspector's report; after all, he had dated Ms. Janet Darville.

Right after lunch, Max had the carriage prepared, and Lucy and I went to take Emily's dress for the necessary adjustments she was so insistent upon. In my opinion, it fit Emily perfectly.

Our driver stopped in front of the Burlington Arcade gallery. We hopped out and asked him to drive around Piccadilly for a bit, as we might take some time. Lucy, having been to the seamstress a few times with Emily, was still dazzled by the sophistication of some shops. Her eyes widened, looking everywhere, attached to nothing.

Upon entering the shop, I felt a chill run down my spine; someone was watching me. I turned around quickly, but saw nothing unusual, just some ladies and a few gentlemen, all very well-dressed, strolling through the gallery corridor. I stayed put for a while, watching and looking in every direction, but it was just an impression.

The seamstress was waiting for us. Emily had sent a message earlier that we would visit right after lunch. She complained a bit about making the adjustments, as she considered that dress her masterpiece. Yet, she was sure Emily would come back to undo the adjustments she had requested. But she did it professionally.

Walking towards the exit of the gallery, the feeling of being watched persisted. I looked from side to side. Nothing. Just people circulating, looking for a shop to enter. We headed for the street, descended the two steps from the central archway of the gallery, and waited for our carriage to arrive. I was alert and Lucy was distracted by the movement of the carriages, oblivious to the anxiety consuming me.

Our carriage arrived. We walked to get in when someone shouted: "Rowena, wait!"

Lucy and I turned around, startled. It was Thomas, coming towards us, walking fast, with labored breaths.

"What are you doing here, Thomas?"

"I was on my way to The Express when I saw George standing in front of the gallery, sneaking peeks inside. I found it odd, a fugitive from the police, here in broad daylight, he was surely up to no good. I decided to get off the carriage because I remembered that your seamstress was at this address. I called out to him, and when he saw me, he ran. I tried to catch up, but he had a carriage waiting for him further ahead. He must have followed you from your house to here."

"When I entered the seamstress's shop, I had the feeling I was being watched. It must have been him. The inspector needs to arrest George as soon as possible, otherwise, my life will turn into a nightmare; I'll always be looking over my shoulder."

"I will accompany you home."

Thomas opened the carriage door, and we got in. Lucy sat next to me, and he sat across from us.

"I'm tired of being watched by criminals. First, it was therapist Cage, now George."

"When did Mr. Cage bother you?"

"Remember when I told you that a man was spying on my window the other day? It was him. I don't understand how he found my address."

"Maybe I know how. As soon as I started at The Express, about two years ago. One of the first stories I did was with therapist Cage, he was at the height of success. I never saw him again and had almost forgotten about him. Maybe on the day of the actress's murder, he recognized me. I didn't identify him because, besides him being masked, he used you as a shield. He definitely investigated who the lady with me was and used as a hostage, finding your address. It's the only plausible explanation."

"Why didn't he watch you as well? After all, we were together at the crime scene."

"Maybe he did spy on me, I just didn't notice. You saw him, otherwise, you wouldn't even know he was spying."

Upon arriving home, I freed the carriage to take Thomas back to The Express. He abandoned his engagement because of George.

Lucy helped Emily try on the dress, and my sister was pleased with the alterations. I went down to talk to my father in his office. I knocked on the door and entered. I told him about my trip to the seamstress and about George's lurking presence. I didn't know what his intentions were, but thanks to Thomas's intervention, everything turned out fine, but I was scared.

"This has to stop. I'll call the inspector; he must station a police officer to watch our house."

Papa wrote a message, called Max, and asked him to deliver it to the inspector as quickly as possible.

I was at my bedroom window, enjoying the dusk as it arrived, bringing the inspector in his black carriage, which looked more like a hearse. All that was missing were the huge black feathers that adorned those vehicles. He descended quickly and knocked sharply on our door knocker. I prepared to go down, knowing my father would soon call for me. Beforehand, I checked on Emily's room, the door was open, and she was focused on her paintings. Emily loved and had a knack for painting. Her landscapes were very realistic. She used to say that my art was music, especially the piano, but I never took it very seriously.

I arrived at the office; the door was open, and the inspector was inside. From his expression, Dr. Robert had given him a hard time. We greeted each other, and I sat down.

"Your father just told me that Mr. George followed you?"

"I didn't actually see him. I just felt someone was watching. Thomas chased him and alerted me. He must have followed me; there's no other way he could have found where I was."

"We have to station a police officer to watch our house, in case he shows up again."

"It would be ideal, Dr. Robert, but we simply don't have enough police officers for that. I was at the Holyheads' today, and the atmosphere there was quite tense. Dr. Henry just got back from his trip, and I had to inform him about Cage's arrest and his wife's involvement in the case. I told him about George and the murders, and even about his daughter Emily's kidnapping. The man was beside himself. He hasn't had news from his son for a while now, and blames his wife's negligence towards their son and home. As for the affair, it was clear he knew about it; they were living a lie for the sake of London society. After the actress's murder, that was the last straw; he made it clear he's planning to leave London."

"Leave London? What do you mean?" Dad asked. "He has a hospital to run."

"I don't know, Doctor. As for George, I'll step up the search and ask the officers to conduct more thorough patrols in that area. I ask Miss Stein to always have company, to avoid giving George Holyhead any opportunities."

"I'll be careful, Inspector."

Mr. Tennyson said his goodbyes, I got up, closed the office door, and sat down again.

"Forgive me for the familiarity, Dad. Are you still taking those mercury pills?"

"We had agreed not to bring up this topic again."

"I know. I would like to make a deal with you."

"A deal?"

"My blood has been proven to have healing powers. It healed Thomas's wound. It cured Emily. I've never been sick. I want you to stop taking those dreadful pills that are causing you harm. Besides, you don't even know if you're sick. If the disease shows up after stopping the medication, I'll give you a blood transfusion, and we'll eradicate it from your body completely. The transfusion worked for Emily; it will work for you too."

"I've already stopped taking them, Rowena, since the day we talked. I appreciate it, my daughter, but I believe I won't need that transfusion"—he gave me a smile—"That's why George is desperate, even without understanding how your blood worked, he coveted it. It's a shame he tried to obtain it the wrong way. With deaths."

"I can understand his pain, but I can't condone the evil he did. He needs to pay for his crimes."

"I feel sorry for Dr. Henry Holyhead. An adulterous wife, a son young and promising but on the brink of madness. I don't even know what to say to him at the hospital, after what George has done to Emily."

"Don't seek him out, let him come to apologize to you."

Leaving my father's office, I felt relieved; he had stopped taking the pills, one less worry on my mind.

Twenty-five

I had developed an obsession with looking out of my bedroom window upon waking up. That morning was no different, a few weeks had passed since George spied on me in Burlington Arcade. I drew the curtains and let the brightness of the beautiful day flood my room. As always, I lingered for a while, watching the square in front of our house. I searched behind trees, bushes, or even among the people walking around for George's face. Like on the other days, there was no sign of George, unless he was camouflaged like a soldier in the trenches.

I grew tired of watching and went down to have my coffee. As I sat at the table, Mary Penny handed me an envelope. It was a letter from Aunt Annie. I opened the letter.

My dear Rowena

I've been reading the newspapers that my beloved Lord William Chapman receives daily from London, and some facts have made me quite anxious. Especially the incident with Emily. I also wrote a little letter to her.

I miss both of you dearly, and I hope to see you soon to clarify the facts when you come to my wedding. Lord William is a major tea importer from India and distributes the product to several countries, including England. The great news is that he is opening an office in New York, as his business has grown significantly in the United States. That's why we're spending some time here in America. Taking advantage of our stay, we will formalize our marriage in this city.

I wrote to father, who despite being his usual grumpy self, has decided to come to the wedding. My brother Robert, I believe, won't be able to come, as I read in the newspapers that Dr. Henry Holyhead has stepped down as head of the Hospital and appointed Robert as his successor. This makes me very happy; my brother has always been a highly skilled doctor, and they've recognized his true value. I asked your grandfather to accompany you two on this trip. He agreed, as it will give him a chance to bond with his granddaughters.

I found out here how I can help you achieve your great dream of becoming a doctor. In Geneva, a small city in New York, there's a medical school, Geneva Medical College, that accepts female students. In London's schools, the archaic notion that we women, despite being intelligent, have frail bodies and stomachs for the practice of medicine persists, not to mention the embarrassment we would feel at seeing naked men, during autopsies and the necessary studies to practice the profession. I believe it will be a while before women are accepted into English medical schools.

Lord William would be honored to host you at our home for the duration of your studies, should you pass the entrance exams of the school, which I believe you will, with flying colors.

From your dear aunt

Annie

As I read each line of the letter, I nibbled on a biscuit and sipped a bit of coffee, so moved by the news. I must have indulged in more treats than ever before. Later, my liver would complain.

I was happy for auntie, it seems she had found her Prince Charming. I was glad that we might go to her wedding, since our grandfather had agreed to take us. I was immensely happy at the possibility of fulfilling my dream of becoming a doctor, like my father. That is, of course, if he would allow me to study so far away. A sadness struck my heart when I thought of Thomas, I would lose him if I went to study in another country. Maybe we would never see each other again. Was it worth the sacrifice of not seeing Thomas for so long? Would he wait for me?

My father was in the library reading the newspaper. I showed him the letter before he left for the hospital. He took the letter and began to read it. I waited on the sofa facing the fireplace, a few embers from the night still crackled, hoping to survive their misfortune. He smiled as he read the letter.

"It seems my sister is happy. I misjudged Lord William. I'll check with father if he's really going to the wedding and if he could take you and Emily, and bring you back to London afterwards. You know I can't leave the country right now. I'm at the beginning of my tenure at the Hospital. I'd love to accompany you, but I can't. However, I shouldn't deprive you of this ceremony which is so important to my sister."

"I'm sorry, father, but what about medical school?"

"That's a tough decision to make right now. It involves a lot of factors, and I don't want to be away from you. The faculty might reject you for being too young. Let's not get our hopes up. Would you be brave enough to live in another country by yourself?"

"It would be a major step in my life, I'm not even sure if I'm ready, but Aunt Annie will be there to support me. I'd like to try."

"I'll think about it. I need time to decide. George is still at large, and that's my biggest concern right now. For now, we'll just make arrangements for you to go to Annie's wedding."

Father handed me the letter, grabbed his newspaper to continue reading. I went up to Emily's room. Lucy was just finishing combing her hair. I mentioned that I had received a letter from Aunt Annie and that she would receive one as well. I talked about the wedding in New York, and that father had allowed us to go. She was happy, but would have preferred it to be in Paris, Auntie's old address, she'd love to visit the City of Light. I didn't show the letter, nor did I bring up the medical school; it was too early to make any decisions. I don't even know if father would let me study that far away.

I went to my room and wrote a note to Thomas, went down, and asked Max to deliver it.

At the agreed-upon time in the afternoon, Thomas showed up. I was sitting on my daydreaming bench, in the small garden of my house. His carriage stopped in front of the gate, and he got down. He radiated a beauty unlike any other day. My heart felt like it was about to burst. I didn't want to admit it, but I loved Thomas, and there was no denying that. He opened the darn iron gate that always squealed, but subdued by Thomas's charms, the gate stayed quiet.

He sat down beside me, held my hands, and pressed his lips against them, and my heart was off to the races.

"Your face looks tense. Why did you call me?"

"Any news from George?"

"No! The police have been surveilling all the Holyhead properties, and no sign of him. I think he's no longer in London. But I believe that's not why you called me here?"

I took the letter from my aunt from my dress pocket and handed it to Thomas. He unfolded the paper and started reading. His eyebrows rose as he finished.

"Do you intend to enroll in this school?"

"Father is against it, but I'd at least like to try. I don't know if I can stay away from you and your wild adventures."

He held my hand and caressed it.

"It's always been your dream. I'd be selfish to ask you to stay, and wait for some change in our laws regarding the admission of females to medical schools."

"I haven't decided anything yet. I don't even know if my father will allow it."

"But your heart is already there, Rowena."

Thomas stood up and walked to open the gate, I ran up to him and we embraced.

The sound of a carriage stopping abruptly next to Thomas's alerted us. The door opened and a frenzied George, wielding a gun, jumped out.

"Don't try anything stupid, Thomas," he said, pointing the gun at Thomas's forehead. From outside the gate.

He opened the gate, still with the gun on Thomas pulled me by the arm, and said:

"Come with me, or he dies, right here," and pointed the gun at my face.

Fearing Thomas might get hurt, I complied. He pushed me into the interior of his carriage and signaled the driver to speed off, with the door still open. I fell onto one of the seats, quickly turned around, and landed a fierce kick with the tip of my boot on his chin. George fell on the opposite bench, and his gun landed on the floor of the carriage. Then, without thinking, I threw myself out of the vehicle, which was picking up speed with the door still open.

As I had dressed up to receive Thomas, I was wearing a dress with multiple layers, which helped cushion my fall. I can honestly say it was far from graceful. Unfortunately, I still ended up with scratches on my arms and face.

Wilkes, who was driving the carriage towards me, slowed down, and Thomas jumped out to help me, while his vehicle continued chasing George. With swift action, Wilkes matched the pace of our horses with George's, forcing them to a halt. The horses rebelled, veering towards the lawns of Garden Square. At the junction where the road met the garden's slope, a small curb caused George's vehicle wheels to lock, overturning the carriage. The driver leaped out just in time to avoid injury.

Thomas and I rushed to look for George. The vehicle had dragged its side along the ground, the horses still trying to rise but were unable due to being tethered. The horrific scene before me shook me to the core; George's head had shattered the window and slammed violently against the ground.

I checked his pulse, finding none. He was dead, his neck broken. A wave of revulsion hit me; no death, no matter how deserved, is acceptable. I took Thomas's hand and we stepped away.

Thomas took out paper and pencil from his pocket, wrote two notes. One for Inspector Tennyson and another for my father and asked Wilker to deliver them.

As we walked home and the coachman unhitched the horses from the overturned carriage, we heard the shrill whistle of a police officer running towards us. Thomas identified himself and asked him to secure the scene until the inspector arrived.

Max was startled to see me disheveled and dirty. The scratches on my face and arms faded, leaving only the grime from the road. I asked him to prepare tea for me and Thomas and to send Lucy to my room. Meanwhile, Thomas would fill him in on what had happened.

I quickly cleaned up, washing my arms and face, and Lucy helped me change my dress and tidy my hair. I went downstairs where Thomas and Emily were waiting for me anxiously in the living room. Thomas had shared with Emily the details about George's death. Concern was evident in her gaze; she wanted to know how I was doing. She examined my face and arms and smiled. The table was already set, and the maid served us. Emily and I merely sipped our tea. Thomas, meanwhile, was ravenous; the adrenaline had left him famished.

Twenty-Six

Inspector and Dr. Robert arrived together. We were waiting for them in the library. Upon seeing that I was well, my father came straight to me. Thomas had summarized what had happened to us in the note. He hugged me so tightly it felt like my fragile ribs would break.

All of us sat down, except Inspector Tennyson decided to remain standing. On his arrival, he was the first to visit the accident site to examine the body and arrange its removal. Thomas and I repeated several times in detail, since George attacked us, until the overturning of his carriage, which resulted in his death. The inspector, in search of someone to blame for George's accident because he came from a wealthy family, accused Wilkes of being responsible for the accident. But when pressed by me, Thomas, and Dr. Robert, he dropped the accusation. Wilkes had merely forced George's carriage to stop. It was the driver of the vehicle who was reckless and didn't comply, causing the accident.

I felt a weight lift off my chest as soon as the inspector left. Finally, this chapter was closed in my life. With George's death, only my father, Emily, and Thomas knew my secret, and they would never tell anyone. Dad went to his study and Emily went up to her room while I said goodbye to Thomas in the garden.

"Now that George is no longer in your way, you are free to go wherever you wish. That includes traveling or studying abroad."

"I wish you could come with me, but I know that it's impossible. You are the eldest son and heir to The Express newspaper. Your life is here in London."

"Your Aunt Annie has also invited my family to the wedding," they might want to go, but I won't be attending. I'd rather say my goodbyes to you here and now. Going to the wedding will only extend my suffering. You know how I feel about you.

Thomas stepped closer, took my hands, looked into my eyes, and touched the depths of my soul, my legs weakened, and I couldn't resist.

"I love you, Thomas. How will I live without you in another country?"

He took my chin between his fingertips, lifted my face, and gave me a chaste kiss on my lips. He opened the gate and left.

It had been a week since Thomas said goodbye. Max was instructing the servants to be careful with our trunks, as they were loaded onto the carriage, and my father was giving final instructions to our grandfather. The steamship journey would be long, but Emily was excited. After the wedding, she would return with Grandpa, and I would stay to attempt the medical school admission exams. Auntie had managed to register me and convinced her brother. Dad, much to his chagrin, had given his permission. I should have been happy, but my heart was in pieces, missing the company of Thomas. He hadn't even come to say goodbye.

We settled into the carriage, Dad was with us, he had decided to see everyone off before we boarded the ship. He signaled to the coachman, and we set off, the horses began to trot, but a boy appeared on the road, emerging from a carriage that was stopped further ahead, positioning himself in the path of our horses with arms wide open, the driver pulled the reins and we stopped. The boy came to my window. It was Bob Little. I opened the carriage door, he handed me a message and a small jewelry box.

I looked around at everyone including my father, who nodded at me, so I opened the letter.

Dear Rowena

I haven't been in touch lately, as I've been trying to find the best solution for both of us. I talked to my father about living in New York for a while. He was hesitant but gave me permission to take a two-year break from the newspaper, which I believe is how long your course is. Using his contacts in America, he also managed to get me a journalist position at the New York Post.

I asked Dr. Robert for his blessing for us to date, informing him that I too would be spending some time in New York. He would only give his blessing if we left here engaged, not just as a couple.

Please open the box.

Yours always,

Thomas Fawcett

My hands were shaking as I opened the box, a beautiful engagement ring sparkled before my eyes. I sensed a figure approaching the still-open door. I lifted my face; it was Thomas.

"So? Do you accept?" he asked loudly.

"Yes! A thousand times yes."

I looked at my father, he nodded, and we left.

Acknowledgements

This work would not exist if the talented Mary Shelley hadn't written the masterpiece Frankenstein, or The Modern Prometheus. This book is a tribute to the author.

Rowena Stein, born in 1831. The year of the character's birth is also a tribute to Mary Shelley, as it was the year the 3rd edition of The Modern Prometheus was published, marking the first time her name appeared in print, giving her the proper credit for her work.

Heartfelt thanks to writer A.Z. Cordenonsi, for his invaluable clarifications on my queries about the Victorian Era.

To the writer, researcher, and owner of the website victorianlondon.org, Lee Jackson who despite being separated by an ocean and language barrier, readily assisted me in detail about this period.

To my wife Graça, for her patience during my anxious spells on those long days of writing when I couldn't find the right words. To my daughter and writer Gika Mendonça for the encouragement, meticulous editing (even when procrastinating) and tips on some aspects of the story. To my son Nilton Jr., a programmer, who helped me with my computer, when it decided to play tricks on me and wouldn't work, and to Frida Maria, my Lhasa apso, for the affectionate licks waking me up when the exhaustion of writing made me sleepy.

Creative Freedoms

Some linguistic and behavioral liberties were taken in relation to the era, to enhance the flow of the story.

All the streets, roads, squares, churches, and hospitals existed during the time the story is set. Today some streets have new names.

I tried to stay as true to the period as possible, in terms of female and male behaviors, clothing, inventions of the time, and modes of transportation. Since this is a work of fiction, I hope you will forgive any inconsistencies.

About the Author

TON EMMES

Painter, illustrator, and writer. Loves pizza, strong coffee, detective noir and westerns.

tonemmes@gmail.com

Instagram

@artistniltonmendonca

Author's Works

Fast and Deadly: An exciting journey to the Old West through a time portal

Pitty is the fourth generation of Mastersons. Four cursed knights have broken free, and her destiny is to send them back to purgatory.

Charming cowboy and manager + Friends in love + Family saga + Sisters' love + Duels + Cursed gunslingers + Magic revolver and cane

Upon inheriting an Old West theme park, Pitty Masterson discovers a time portal that takes her back to 1878, where she meets her legendary great-great-grandfather, Bat Masterson.

With the help of John Blackstone, the charming cowboy who runs the park, Pitty embarks on a dangerous mission to rescue her sister from the clutches of demonic gunslingers.

Will the power of love and courage be enough to overcome the fate of these two sisters?

A different kind of western with a touch of romance.

Pitty will have to live in the past: is it worse to die in it?

Soul Thieves

It was a time when everyone knew when they would die; a chip was implanted in their nervous systems, with their death dates. Claudio Clocker didn't want to die. He was young, handsome, and healthy, yet had only a few months to live. Thus, he became a soul thief, capable of breaking the encryption of the implants and stealing people's lifespans, until a seductive redhead appeared...